The Incomparable

The Earl sat down on the side of the bed. "And now, Rita," he said. "What are we going to do about us?"

Amorita looked at him in surprise.

"I mean," the Earl said, "that I won you in competition, and now I am going to tell you what I intend to do about you . . ."

"I . . . I do not . . . understand . . . what you . . . are saying!" Amorita protested.

A Camfield Novel of Love
by Barbara Cartland

———

"Barbara Cartland's novels are all distinguished by their intelligence, good sense, and good nature. . . ."

— ROMANTIC TIMES

"Who could give better advice on how to keep your romance going strong than the world's most famous romance novelist, Barbara Cartland?"

— THE STAR

D1267932

Camfield Place,
Hatfield
Hertfordshire,
England

Dearest Reader,

Camfield Novels of Love mark a very exciting era of my books with Jove. They have already published nearly two hundred of my titles since they became my first publisher in America, and now all my original paperback romances in the future will be published exclusively by them.

As you already know, Camfield Place in Hertfordshire is my home, which originally existed in 1275, but was rebuilt in 1867 by the grandfather of Beatrix Potter.

It was here in this lovely house, with the best view in the county, that she wrote *The Tale of Peter Rabbit*. Mr. McGregor's garden is exactly as she described it. The door in the wall that the fat little rabbit could not squeeze underneath and the goldfish pool where the white cat sat twitching its tail are still there.

I had Camfield Place blessed when I came here in 1950 and was so happy with my husband until he died, and now with my children and grandchildren, that I know the atmosphere is filled with love and we have all been very lucky.

It is easy here to write of love and I know you will enjoy the Camfield Novels of Love. Their plots are definitely exciting and the covers very romantic. They come to you, like all my books, with love.

Bless you,

Barbara Cartland

CAMFIELD NOVELS OF LOVE
by Barbara Cartland

A NEW CAMFIELD NOVEL OF LOVE BY

BARBARA CARTLAND

The Incomparable

JOVE BOOKS, NEW YORK

THE INCOMPARABLE

A Jove Book / published by arrangement with
the author

PRINTING HISTORY
Jove edition / January 1995

All rights reserved.
Copyright © 1995 by Barbara Cartland.
Cover artwork copyright © 1995 by Fiord Forlag A/S.
This book may not be reproduced in whole
or in part, by mimeograph or any other means,
without permission. For information address:
The Berkley Publishing Group, 200 Madison Avenue,
New York, New York 10016.

ISBN: 0-515-11531-2

A JOVE BOOK®
Jove Books are published by The Berkley Publishing Group,
200 Madison Avenue, New York, New York 10016.
JOVE and the "J" design are trademarks
belonging to Jove Publications, Inc.

PRINTED IN THE UNITED STATES OF AMERICA

10 9 8 7 6 5 4 3 2 1

Author's Note

IN the Regency, the Bucks and *Beaux* and the fashionable young Lords, when they were not gambling and losing a fortune on cards, spent their time having *affaires de coeur* with the Beauties of the *Beau Ton* and pursuing those who were known as the *Cyprians*, or the *"Fashionable Impures."*

If there was one particularly outstanding amongst them, she was known as *"The Incomparable."*

They had individual names such as the "White Doe," the "Mocking Bird," "Venus Mendicant."

Their shop window was a Box at the Opera or a separate Box for the Season at the King's Theatre in the Haymarket.

The Noblemen would come round to pay their respects while the performance was taking place, despite the fact that their wives were in the audience.

In fact, to quote one of the best reference books of the time:

> *"The amorous, idle gentlemen of*
> *the Regency were totally unashamed of*
> *their uninhibited lust for sexual pleasure.*
> *They were hell-bent on living high with*
> *an absolute disregard for the consequences."*

They could be excused from being in any way extraordinary when the Prince himself was notorious for his Mistresses, and his brother the Duke of York promised Mary Anne Clarke 1,000 pounds a month.

The most important of the Cyprians were Harriette Wilson and her sisters.

Harriette was, in fact, the idol of half the men of the *Beau Monde*. She had been born in Mayfair in Shepherd Market and at the age of fifteen had run away with the Earl of Craven.

When she was tired of him she fell into the arms of Lord Melbourne's eldest son, the Honorable Frederick Lamb. But he kept her short of money and she was rescued by the Marquis of Lorne, later Duke of Argyll, who was extremely rich.

This inevitably brought her to the top of her

profession, where she remained until she married.

She was undoubtedly *"An Incomparable"* without a peer, but there were always new faces and new Cyprians striving to climb the ladder to the top.

chapter one

1820

THE Earl of Eldridge walked up the steps and in through the front-door of Whites Club.

There was a pause before the Porter said:

"G'mornin', M'Lord. It's nice t' see you back!"

The Earl smiled.

It was traditional that the Porters of Whites should know all its members, and he had been away for a long time.

"I am glad to be back, Johnson," he said.

He was pleased with himself that he had remembered the Porter's name.

Handing over his tall hat, he walked through the door into the Morning-Room.

He took a quick glance at the bow-window at which Beau Brummell had, before he was exiled from England, held court.

Then he saw the men he was looking for at

the far end of the room.

There were four of them, and as he walked towards them they stared at him in astonishment, then gave a shout.

"Roydin!" they exclaimed. "Is it really you?"

They jumped to their feet and held out their hands.

The Earl shook the hands of four of his best friends, with three of whom he had been at Eton.

"Where have you been all this time?" James Ponsonby asked.

"I have been in the country, Jimmy," the Earl said, "propping up my leaking roof and trying to save my pensioners from starvation."

He spoke with a note of bitterness in his voice.

Then he added in a different tone:

"But now—it is all over—completely and absolutely—all over!"

He spoke the last words slowly, and his friends stared at him.

"What do you mean by that?" one of them asked.

The Earl took a deep breath before he answered:

"I am rich! I am unexpectedly, extraordinarily, and unbelievably rich!"

For a moment there was complete silence.

Then, as they all began to talk at once, the Earl held up his hand.

"For the Lord's sake, give me a drink. I need

it! And if you want to know the truth, I am in a state of shock!"

He laughed, and before anyone could speak he called a Steward.

"Two bottles of your finest champagne—no—three—and hurry!"

The Steward hastened to obey him, and the Earl sat back in one of the brown leather chairs, saying:

"Give me time. I will tell you everything in a minute, but—I can hardly believe it myself!"

His friends were all aware that, when the tenth Earl of Eldridge had died, his son had inherited the title together with a mountain of debts.

He had left London to cope with an Estate that had been neglected and a Castle which was in urgent need of repair.

When they did not hear from the new Earl, they guessed that he could not return to London because he could not afford it.

With surprising swiftness the Steward brought a bottle of champagne in an ice-cooler.

He filled up five glasses and the Earl drank his in one gulp.

Then he said:

"Another bottle, and keep it as cool as you can."

"Very good, M'Lord."

The Earl finished his champagne, then said:

"I know you are all curious, so now I will tell

you what has happened."

"If you are really rich," Charles Raynam replied, "I can only imagine that you have struck gold in one of your fields, or found a Royal treasure in one of the attics."

"That is what I prayed might happen," the Earl said as he laughed, "but, I assure you, there is nothing in the attics except rats, and all my fields contain are weeds!"

"Then what has happened?" Jimmy Ponsonby asked. "For goodness' sake, Roydin, do not keep us in suspense. We are dying of curiosity!"

The Earl, however, put out his glass to be refilled and one of his friends obligingly did so.

"I do not know if you remember," he said, "but my Father's brother was a disagreeable man whom I seldom saw, except at Funerals. He disliked the family—unless they were dead— so he moved to Northumberland and bought a house there."

"I remember him coming down to Eton once," Jimmy said, "and when he left, he tipped you sixpence, which I thought was the meanest thing I have ever known!"

"That was like Uncle Lionel," the Earl agreed, "and, while my Father was too open-handed and a spendthrift, he became exactly the opposite—a miser!"

The Earl sipped his second glass of champagne.

Then, realising his friends were waiting, he went on:

"I was notified a fortnight ago that my Uncle had died and I received a letter from his Solicitors informing me that, as he had made me his heir, they wanted to see me immediately."

He paused and then continued:

"I did not think it would be worth the journey to London. However, I prayed he had left me something, if only his best wishes, which would cost him nothing."

The Earl took another sip of his champagne and, before anybody could speak, he went on:

"In fact—he left me—everything he possessed!"

"Everything?" Charlie asked. "How much is that?"

The Earl paused, as if it were difficult to reply. Then he said slowly:

"A little over—three-million pounds!"

There was an audible gasp from his friends.

Then they all began again to talk at once.

"How is it possible he would do that?"

"Why had you no idea of it?"

"Why?—Why?—Why?"

The Earl held up his hand.

"I know what you are asking, and I can tell you quite simply—he skimped and saved all his life, investing in various Companies which he always investigated very carefully."

He paused, sipping his champagne, and then continued:

"He also had some holdings in America which have turned up trumps, while the money he accumulated year after year has increased and increased."

"I have never heard anything so exciting!" Jimmy exclaimed. "Congratulations, Roydin! And if it was not my good luck to become a Midas, then I am delighted that it should be yours!"

"Thank you, Jimmy," the Earl answered, "and I promise you one thing—I will never forget my old friends."

He drank a little more champagne before he said:

"In fact, on my way here I was thinking of how I could reward you for your friendship over the years, and I have a special plan to which I hope you will agree."

Before he could say any more, three young men who had just entered the room came up to shake him by the hand.

"It is good to see you, Roydin," they said. "What the devil have you been doing with yourself? We have missed you!"

"I am back," the Earl replied, "and now I am staying! Sit down and let me tell you what I intend to do."

They sat down.

The Earl filled their glasses with champagne and ordered another bottle.

He told the new arrivals of his good luck.

Then he asked:

"How many are we?"

"Ten," Charlie replied, glancing round at his friends.

"Then I think we should be two more," the Earl said. "It would be unlucky to be thirteen!"

"You have no cause to talk about bad luck," somebody said, laughing.

" 'Easy come, easy go,' " Jimmy Ponsonby quoted, "and whatever it is that Roydin has in mind, I think twelve is quite enough."

As he spoke, two more men came into the room, and he called them over.

One of them, the Earl noticed, was Sir Mortimer Martin, for whom he had never particularly cared.

Nevertheless, he greeted him and said nothing more.

With Sir Mortimer was another Baronet called Edward Howe.

Harry, as he had always been called, was a great friend of the Earl's.

The Earl sat down beside him, saying as he did so:

"I am glad you are here, Harry. I was hoping to see you while I was in London."

"And I have been hoping to see you!" Harry

replied. "How could you have stayed away for so long?"

"It was not a case of wanting to," the Earl answered, "as I have just been explaining to our friends. But listen to what I have planned to amuse you and to express my gratitude for all the years we have been together."

The men had already filled up their glasses.

Now they were sitting forward in their chairs so as not to miss a word of what the Earl was about to say.

"I thought one of you would ask me," he began, "what I want, now that I am rich. Well, I am going to tell you. I want the most beautiful 'Cyprians' in London, I want the finest horses obtainable, and I want to give a party at the Castle to which you are all invited."

There was a lot of laughter at this, and one or two clapped.

"The first should be easy now that you are so rich!" one of them remarked.

"As I have to get the Castle ready to entertain you," the Earl replied, "I have no time to seek out the Cyprians—that is your job."

"What do you mean by that?" Charlie asked.

"To-day is Monday," the Earl said. "I suggest that you come to Elde Castle on Friday, each bringing with you a Cyprian whom you consider is the most beautiful in London."

"That will be Daisy," Jimmy remarked.

"On the contrary," Charlie snapped. "Lou-Lou can beat her into a cocked hat!"

He spoke aggressively, then other men joined in, saying:

"Mavis is superior to both those mentioned."

Others named Milly, Amy, and Doris.

They were all arguing, until the Earl said:

"Now, listen, because I intend to do it my way."

"What does that mean?" Charlie enquired.

"It means," the Earl replied, "that I want each of you to bring the Cyprian you consider the most beautiful, and we will have a parade. The man who brings the girl who gains the most votes will win a prize of a thousand pounds."

"A thousand pounds?" Jimmy gasped.

"That is what I said," the Earl replied, "and the girl will be given a present that glitters."

They were silent in sheer surprise, and he continued:

"There will also be a second and a third prize, just as there will be in the races."

"What races?" someone asked.

"My Father, in one of his more extravagant moments," the Earl explained, "built a race-course. It is a little rough, as it has not been used for a year or two."

He paused and continued:

"But it will be ready by Saturday, and you can

either ride your own horses, or I will provide them for you. I hope by then to have some excellent horse-flesh in my stable! Thank God, they at least are still standing."

"And what are the prizes for the races?" one of his friends asked.

"The same as for the Cyprians—a thousand pounds for the winner of each race, and there will be four. Five hundred pounds for the second, and three hundred and fifty for whoever comes in third."

"This all sounds very exciting!" Jimmy exclaimed. "One thing, Roydin, living in the country has not ruined your brain! You were always the ring-leader of every prank we ever played at Eton."

"And at Oxford, for that matter!" Charlie joined in.

"I thought it would amuse you," the Earl said. "Now, before I return to the country, you will have to help me find some decent horses of my own."

Again everybody began to talk at once.

Out of the chaos the Earl gathered that the Marquess of Montepart was "below hatches," and selling off his Stud.

There was also a Sale at Tattersalls that very afternoon.

He rose to his feet.

"We will go to Tattersalls," he said, "so the

sooner we have Luncheon, the better, and I hope you will be my guests."

He smiled at his friends and then continued:

"I cadged meals from you all in the past. It is now my great pleasure to be able to repay your hospitality."

They laughed at this, and moved towards the Dining-Room.

The Earl sent a message to the Chef to tell him to serve the best and most expensive meal he had ever eaten.

It was an enjoyable Luncheon at which everybody was laughing and shouting to make themselves heard.

They then drove off in various Phaetons to Tattersalls Salerooms.

Here the Earl purchased six outstanding horses.

He then asked Charlie to buy him several more the following day if he thought they were good enough.

"You know Montepart," he went on, "so see if any of his horses are worth buying before the Sale, at whatever price he asks."

"I will do that," Charlie replied.

Lord Raynam was older than the Earl and one of his best friends.

He was a member of the Jockey Club and an acknowledged authority on race-horses.

"I trust your judgement because I consider

your taste is similar to mine where horses are concerned," the Earl said, "and if everything at the Castle is to be ready by Friday, I must return home immediately."

He looked round at the friends who encircled him and said:

"I think you all know your way to the Castle. I shall expect you early on Friday afternoon and, of course, will be ready to greet the lovely ladies you will be bringing with you."

"I suppose they are essentially a part of our invitation?" someone asked.

"Of course," the Earl replied, "and you will not be admitted without them."

There was laughter at this.

Then two of the Earl's friends began quarrelling as to who should bring a girl called "Molly."

They each believed she was the undisputed "Incomparable" of the moment.

The Earl turned towards the gate, and as he did so, found Harry Howe standing beside him.

"I shall back you, Harry," he said in a low voice, "to win one of the races. Unless times have changed, you were always one of the best riders I have ever seen."

"Thank you, Roydin," Harry replied, "but I have not had anything decent to ride for some time."

"Every horse in my stable is at your disposal," the Earl said.

He put his hand on his friend's shoulder.

"I have never forgotten the fun we used to have at Oxford, when we broke all the rules and got away with it!"

Harry laughed.

"I often wondered how we were lucky enough not to be sent down."

"We survived," the Earl said quietly, "and that, Harry, is what we both are—survivors!"

He did not say any more because Sir Mortimer Martin came up to say:

"Congratulations, Roydin! There is no one who deserves more than you to have a good run of luck!"

"Thank you," the Earl replied. "I assure you, I am very, very grateful to the Gods, or whoever is looking after me."

Sir Mortimer made no reply, but Harry, watching him, thought he saw a glint of jealousy in his eye.

The Earl, however, was already stepping into the Phaeton in which he had driven to the Salesrooms.

His friends noticed it was somewhat old, and in need of a coat of paint.

The two horses drawing it were also past their best.

The Earl had travelled in it to visit the Salerooms.

But they were certain the next time they saw him, the vehicle he drove would be very different.

The Earl picked up the reins and waved his hand.

His friends cheered him and threw their hats in the air as he drove away.

"He has the Devil's own luck!" Sir Mortimer exclaimed as they watched the Phaeton until it was out of sight.

"No-one deserves it more than Roydin," Charlie said sharply. "It has worried me more than I can tell you to know that this last year he could not afford to come to London. Now, thank heavens, we will see more of him again, as we used to do in the past."

There was a murmur of agreement from all the others.

Then Jimmy was walking towards his own Phaeton with Charlie beside him.

"If there is one man I cannot stand," he said when they were out of ear-shot, "it is Mortimer Martin. I cannot think how he has been included in this party!"

"He came to join us when Roydin was telling us what had happened, then somehow became included."

"That was a mistake, if you ask me," Jimmy said. "I think he is a nasty piece of work and I know at the moment he is gambling heavily—

more heavily than he can afford."

"I thought that the other night when I was in the Club," Charlie said.

They drove on a little way before Jimmy asked:

"Who are you planning to bring to take part in the Cyprian contest?"

"Need you ask?" Charlie replied.

"No, I suppose not," Jimmy said, "and I will have to make do with Lou-Lou. She looks extremely attractive, especially in the evening."

Charlie laughed.

"They all look better in the evening than when they first wake up!"

Jimmy made a somewhat lewd remark, at which they both laughed heartily.

At the same time, as they drove on, they were both considering privately how they could produce a Cyprian who would outshine all the others.

Harry Howe had refused several offers of a lift because he was not returning to St. James's Street.

Instead, he took a Hackney Carriage and drove down to Chelsea.

Not far from the Hospital that had been inaugurated by Nell Gwynn, there was an extremely attractive house with which he was very familiar.

When he rang the bell the door was opened by

a parlourmaid in a frilly cap and a white apron.

"Ow, 'tis you, Sir Edward!" she exclaimed, bobbing a curtsy. "I wondered if we'd be seein' you at Luncheon time."

"I am late," Harry said briefly.

He walked into the Sitting-Room, which was on the Ground Floor.

An extremely pretty young woman jumped up as he appeared and held out her arms.

"Harry!" she exclaimed. "I thought you'd forgotten me!"

"I am sorry, Milly," Harry answered. "I intended to come to Luncheon, but something happened which prevented me from doing so."

He put his arms around her but he had not yet kissed her.

Before he could do so, she asked curiously:

"What has happened?"

"I will tell you in a minute," Harry answered.

He kissed her, holding her close against him until with a little gesture she extricated herself.

"I'm curious!"

"You will be even more so when I tell you what has happened," Harry said.

Milly sat down on the sofa and Harry sat beside her.

He told her how he had been in Whites Club and how the Earl of Eldridge had come in with the fabulous news that he had inherited a large fortune.

"Oh, Harry!" Milly breathed. "If only it had been you!"

"That is what I thought too," Harry said. "But listen, because you will enjoy what is coming next."

He told her that the Earl was giving a party at which all his friends had to bring the prettiest Cyprian they knew.

He told her that the prize for producing the most beautiful was 1,000 pounds.

The girl herself would receive "something that glittered."

He used the Earl's words and added:

"Which means, of course, 'diamonds!' "

Milly's eyes lit up.

"Oh, Harry, that sounds wonderful!"

"It will be," Harry said, "especially as I am sure I will win the races too."

"And is there a prize for that as well?" Milly asked.

"Yes, it is the same as for the Cyprians," Harry answered.

"And when does the party take place?" Milly enquired.

"Next Friday," Harry replied.

Milly's face fell.

"Oh, not next Friday!"

"Why not? What is wrong?" Harry enquired.

"The Baron's coming back that evening."

"Oh, no! I do not believe it!" Harry said.

"It's true," Milly assured him. "I heard from him this morning."

"But, surely," Harry said, "you can find an excuse to come with me to Elde Castle?"

Milly shook her head.

"You know that's impossible."

There was silence.

Harry knew as well as Milly, whom he had known for three years, that she was under the protection of Baron von Waltermer.

The Baron, who was an exceedingly rich man, had made his home in England for over ten years.

Because he was very clever, he was involved in many new technical companies, and was accepted more or less as an English citizen.

Generous when it suited him, he had provided Milly with a house in Chelsea.

He had also given her a carriage and two horses as well as servants to look after her.

She was undoubtedly the best-dressed Cyprian in the whole of the *Beau Monde*.

What was more, the Baron never went away without bringing her back a present of jewellery.

Even the smallest of them would have been impossible for Harry to afford.

But it was an accepted rule that when a Cyprian was under a Gentleman's "protection," she was not available to anybody else.

It was only because Milly had known Harry

for such a long time that she broke the rule where he was concerned.

She also knew it would be impossible for him to keep her in luxury as the Baron did.

"I'm sorry, Harry," she said now, and her voice was completely sincere.

"It is all right, Milly," he said philosophically, "it is not your fault."

"I'm sure you will be able to find someone else to go with you."

"No-one who looks like you," he answered, "and if it comes to that, I know of no-one apart from you who would get a second look from the other members in the party."

Milly kissed him, but she knew it was poor comfort at the moment.

"I think I had better go back to the Club and see what is happening," Harry said.

"Please stay for dinner?"

He shook his head.

"I will come to-morrow, if I can," he said. "In the meantime, I need to think, and try to find a solution."

"Oh, Harry, if it had been any other week, I could have managed it, but when the Baron's been away for so long, he will be expecting me to be waiting for him eagerly."

"I know, I know!" Harry said testily. "Do not make it worse, Milly. It all comes back to the same thing—that I am a poor man, thankful for the crumbs that fall from the rich man's table."

"I do not like you calling me a crumb!" Milly said. "At the same time, I am sorry, Harry . . . very . . . sorry."

She said it again and again before finally Harry left her.

He drove back in a Hackney Carriage which he picked up at the end of the road.

As he did so, he told himself it was the most unfortunate thing that could possibly happen to him.

He went to his lodgings in Half Moon Street which was a prestigious address, although he occupied only one room in the attic.

As he climbed the steep stairs he was thinking how pleasant it would be if he could be housed in the large, high-ceilinged rooms on the floors below.

Then, as he opened the door to his bedroom, he saw to his astonishment there was somebody there.

She was looking out over the roof-tops and turned as he came in.

"Amorita!" he exclaimed. "What are you doing here?"

She ran towards him.

"Oh, Harry, I am so glad you have come back! I was afraid I might have to wait for ages and ages for you."

"Why are you in London?" Harry asked.

"I have bad news," his sister replied.

"What is it?" Harry enquired.

"Nanny has to have an operation. I have just taken her to the Hospital, and Dr. Graham has arranged for a really good Surgeon to attend her. But, Harry, it is going to cost at least—a hundred pounds!"

Harry gave an exclamation.

"A hundred pounds? We do not have a hundred pounds!"

"I know, I know!" Amorita said. "But we cannot let poor Nanny die, and she is already in a great deal of pain."

Harry put his hand up to his forehead.

"Why did this have to happen now?" he asked desperately.

"Nanny has been with us ever since we were children," Amorita replied, "and now that Mama and Papa are dead, there is nobody else to love us as she does."

"I know that," Harry said, "but I have just had one blow, and this is another!"

"What was the first?" his sister asked curiously.

Harry sat down on the bed.

"You will not believe my bad luck," he said, "and I thought two hours ago that I had a chance of winning two thousand pounds."

"Two thousand pounds?" Amorita exclaimed. "How could you possibly win so much?"

Because it was difficult in the circumstances to tell his sister exactly what had occurred, he said slowly:

"My friend Roydin Eldridge came into Whites Club to-day with the marvellous news that he has come into a fortune."

He went on to explain that the Earl wanted to reward his friends for supporting him when he was poor.

Then he said:

"There will be races at Elde Castle, the prize for the winner being a thousand pounds, and there is another thousand for the man who can produce the prettiest Cyprian at the party."

It was here that Harry was interrupted as Amorita asked:

"What is a 'Cyprian?' "

A little late, Harry realised to whom he was speaking.

After a few seconds' hesitation he replied:

"An—actress."

"Oh, I see!" Amorita remarked.

"I have a friend who would have played the part perfectly," Harry went on. "Unfortunately, she cannot accompany me on that day."

"But, surely, you can find somebody else?" his sister asked.

Harry made a helpless gesture with his hand.

"Quite frankly, I do not know of anyone and, because I am so poor, I cannot afford one."

There was silence as he rose to his feet.

"Why did this have to happen to me?" he asked. "What have I done to deserve such appalling bad luck!"

He walked to the window and with his back to the room said:

"If I cannot produce a Cyprian, I cannot go to the party, and that means I will not get the chance of winning any of the races! Dammit all! The Devil himself could not think of anything worse!"

He spoke furiously.

Then a soft, hesitating little voice behind him asked:

"Why . . . why could I . . . not come with you?"

chapter two

HARRY slowly turned and looked at his sister in astonishment.

"You?" he questioned. "Of course not!"

"But, why ... why not?" Amorita asked. "After all, nobody knows I have not been on the stage, and I can say I am trying to get a part."

Harry hesitated, trying to find the right words. Finally he said:

"You are a Lady, Amorita, and the women with whom you would associate are not."

"I do not see that it matters what they are," Amorita said softly. "What matters is that I would be with you so that you can go to the party, and win a race."

She gave a little sob before she went on:

"We cannot let Nanny ... die ... she has to

have an ... operation ... and if you did win a thousand pounds, think what we could do to the Castle ... pay the wages owing to the Briggses, who have not received their proper money for months!"

Amorita was pleading so fervently that now a tear ran down her cheek.

"Oh, for Heaven's sake, Amorita, do not upset yourself!" Harry exclaimed. "I am feeling bad about it myself without you making it worse."

"I am ... trying to ... make it ... better," Amorita said tearfully.

Harry did not answer, and after a moment she went on:

"I cannot see why I cannot play the part of an out-of-work actress! After all, you say I am a Lady. But it is not written in flames of fire all over my body!"

Harry gave a choked laugh.

"It is no use, Amorita," he said. "I cannot take you to a party where no Lady would go, and if it were known that I had taken my sister there, not only would you be ostracized by Society, but I would very likely be thrown out of my Club."

"I do not believe it!" Amorita exclaimed. "As for me being thrown out of Society, since I have never been to a Ball or one dance, no-one could throw me out anyway."

"Now, listen ..." Harry began, but his sister went on:

"The only thing I must have will be some decent clothes, and as I cannot afford any, I shall have to try and borrow some, but I cannot think . . . from . . . whom."

Harry turned back towards the window.

"That would not present any difficulty," he said. "I could borrow those."

Amorita jumped up from the chair in which she was sitting and joined him at the window.

"You mean . . . you will take . . . me with you?"

"I know it is something I should not do," Harry answered, "and something that would make Papa very angry. But, God knows, I can think of no other way of raising a thousand pounds, and Roydin has offered me the pick of all his new horses."

"Well, there you are!" Amorita said. "He knows you will win, and I know you will win, so, Harry, you cannot refuse to try. Think of . . . Nanny."

The tears were back in her eyes as she went on:

"Since . . . Mama died . . . Nanny has been the only . . . person who really . . . loves us. How can we let her suffer and die . . . without the . . . operation?"

"All right, all right!" Harry sighed. "You win! But for Heaven's sake, Amorita, do not breathe a word of this to anyone—do you understand?

No-one must ever know that you are my sister."

Amorita put her hands round his neck.

"I love you, Harry," she said, "and you know that I would never do anything to hurt you or damage your name."

She sighed before she continued:

"But we cannot go on just slowly . . . starving while the Castle falls . . . down around us until in . . . the end we shall have . . . nowhere to . . . sleep."

She kissed him, then, as she moved a little, he put up his hand to his forehead.

"I must be mad," he said, "but I cannot think of any other way."

"Well, that is one problem solved," Amorita said. "But, Harry, you will have to find me some suitable clothes."

"I will do that."

"I imagine you will ask the lady who could not go with you," Amorita suggested.

"That is true," Harry admitted, "but she is not a Lady, and you are not to talk about her."

"I am talking only to you about her," Amorita said.

"And I am the only person you must talk to at the party. You are to stay by me, pay no attention to what any other man says to you, and most important of all, you are not to talk to the other women there."

"All right," Amorita said grudgingly. "You

can give me your instructions at the last minute, but now I want you to come with me to see Nanny and tell the Hospital that you will pay for her operation."

"And if I do not win, I will shoot myself!" Harry said.

Amorita laughed.

"Now you are being melodramatic! You know perfectly well that you will win a race if you are on a decent horse. And there must be one in the Earl's stables which you would rather ride than any others."

"I shall know better when I have seen them," Harry said, "so we had better be punctual in getting there."

"How far is it?" Amorita asked.

"About fifteen miles from us," he replied. "But with the old horses, which are all we have left, it will take hours."

"We will leave in plenty of time," Amorita answered finally.

She moved away from him to pick up her hand-bag which she had left in the chair in which she had been sitting.

Harry watched her.

Then he said:

"You are quite, quite sure, Amorita, that we should do this? I have been a poor substitute for Papa when it comes to breaking in horses, but I know he would be horrified."

Amorita smiled.

"You have been marvellous! It was not your fault that we could not find a really good Yearling at the last two sales we attended. But I have a feeling that now our luck is changing."

Harry sighed.

Their Father, the Baronet, had been accidentally killed when he was breaking in a horse.

He had been hoping to sell it for a large profit, which was the way in which Sir Arnold Howe had managed to live in comparative comfort.

Howe Castle had been in the family for three centuries.

Unfortunately, none of the Howes who had inherited it had ever had a great deal of money.

When Sir Arnold came into the title and the small Estate, he had been the first member of the family to be able to make some.

The reason was that he had an extraordinary way of controlling horse-flesh.

The wildest horse became docile and obedient when he trained it.

After he married, he and his wife were perfectly happy buying and selling horses and living in a tumble-down Castle.

Sir Arnold did so well that he could afford to send his son to Eton, then to Oxford.

During the war, however, the best horses were taken by the Army.

Then he found it difficult to obtain the Yearlings he needed.

It was equally difficult to find exceptional horses which he could train and sell for really large sums.

They were, however, completely happy.

It had never worried Lady Howe, who was very beautiful but seldom went to parties.

Because her gowns were not fashionable, when her husband had to go to London, he went alone.

It was only when Amorita was older that she worried.

How could her daughter, who was growing very like her, ever have a chance of meeting the right sort of man to marry?

Lady Howe was well aware that her son, Harry, when he went to London, moved amongst the *Beaux* and Bucks who were to be found in St. James's Street.

But Harry seldom brought anyone home.

This was because he could not entertain his friends as lavishly as they entertained him.

After Sir Arnold's death, which was not his fault, but just bad luck, Harry knew he had to try and follow in his Father's footsteps.

He had to find the money necessary for the upkeep of the Castle.

He had to pay the servants, and buy the food for what was left of his family.

It was perhaps because she worried so much about the situation that Lady Howe became so ill.

She caught a cold in the winter, which turned to pneumonia, and she died.

Lady Howe had been worrying, too, about Amorita.

Perhaps by some miracle, she could have a Season in London when she reached the age of eighteen.

Instead of which, there were the Funeral expenses to be met.

Harry had therefore to sell a horse more cheaply than he had intended.

Brother and sister found themselves alone in the Castle with the roof slowly collapsing about their ears.

Harry had broken in one horse which he had taken to London and sold for a reasonable sum.

He was aware, however, that nearly every penny was needed to pay the bills of the tradesmen in the village in which they lived.

He also had to provide other horses, which he could break in.

He had gone to Whites hoping there would be somebody there who would tell him they had some foals that needed bringing up to scratch and would pay him for doing so.

As he walked into the Club, he hoped he was not wasting his time.

It had seemed like a gift from Heaven to find his friend Roydin Eldridge offering enormous sums for a race he felt quite certain he could win.

The condition, however, had been that he could come only if he was accompanied by a Cyprian.

He had been sure when he had left Tattersalls for Chelsea that Milly would go with him.

That the Baron was coming back at precisely the wrong moment was a shattering piece of bad luck.

Now the only chance of him having enough money to pay for their Nurse's operation was to take his sister, of all people, to Elde Castle.

"I ought not to do it—it is wrong," he was saying to himself.

Then, looking at his sister as if for the first time, he realised that she was very lovely.

It was not in the same way that the Cyprians looked, with their flashing eyes and painted faces, or their traditional charms which they could turn on and off like a tap.

Amorita was very fair; in fact, her hair was the colour of the sun when it first rose in the East.

She had the traditionally English pink-and-white complexion.

Yet her skin was whiter than any Harry had ever seen, except on his Mother.

Her eyes were very large and seemed almost

to fill her small, pointed face.

But instead of being blue, they were the pale green of a stream, flecked with the sun.

"She is lovely!" Harry said to himself in surprise, as if he had just discovered it.

He knew then that it would be a crime to put her amongst men who would pursue her for reasons he dared not think about.

"Why are you staring at me, Harry?" Amorita asked unexpectedly.

"I am wondering what we can do to make you look like an—an a-actress," Harry said, stumbling over the words.

"You need not worry about that," Amorita answered. "You remember when we acted in the Nativity Play at Christmas, Mama showed me how to make up the cast myself. Everyone was very complimentary about how well I had done it."

"What did you do with the paint and powder?" Harry asked.

"It is at home somewhere," Amorita answered. "I will find it, do not worry."

"You will have to wear it all the time you are at Elde Castle," her brother said.

"Is that the name of the Earl's Castle?" Amorita enquired. "And if he has a Castle, so have you, Harry. I am sure that is an omen of Good Luck!"

"It will be bad luck if he discovers who you are," Harry snapped, "so listen, Amorita, you must go home, and I will come to-morrow."

He thought for a moment before he went on:

"I hope to bring you the clothes you are to wear, and you can practise with the make-up you used at Christmas until you look exactly like an actress. Do you understand?"

Amorita nodded.

"Of course I understand," she said. "I think you are making a great fuss about nothing! After all, if, as you say, all the other women taking part are accomplished actresses, no-one is going to worry about me!"

Harry hoped that was true.

At the same time, he felt as if he were sinking deeper and deeper into a dark pool which would eventually swallow him up.

"Now we have to go and see Nanny," Amorita said, "and you must talk to the Surgeon, who is rather a frightening man."

"All right," Harry agreed. "But after that you must return at once to the country."

He saw his sister look at him questioningly and explained:

"No-one in London must see you with me looking as you do now. Otherwise they will know when we arrive at the Castle that you are not who you are pretending to be."

"Of course, that is sensible," Amorita said. "Anyway, judging by what I saw when I came here, nobody will look twice at me."

She looked down at her shabby gown as she spoke, and Harry felt ashamed of himself.

Surely he could make enough money to give his sister at least one decent gown?

He admitted silently that he was not as good at breaking in horses as his Father had been.

They went to the Hospital, where they were received by a hard-faced Matron.

Then, after she learned that Harry had a title, she became more affable.

She showed them the room which Nanny would occupy all by herself.

"It's only a little more expensive than being in a Ward," she said, "but I'm sure it is something you would want for the person who has looked after you ever since you were children."

With just a slight hesitation, Harry agreed.

They went to find Nanny.

She was being given a cup of tea in the Waiting-Room, where patients were left until the Doctors could see them.

Amorita put her arms around her old Nurse and kissed her.

"It is all right, Nanny darling," she said. "Harry is arranging for you to have a delightful room all to yourself, and they say that Sir William Thompson is the finest Surgeon in London! In fact, he looks after His Royal Highness."

"Then I hopes he looks after me properly," Nanny said.

Harry laughed.

"I am sure you will tell him so sharply if he does not, and he will do as he is told."

Nanny smiled. Then she said:

"It'll be costly, Master Harry, and I'd just as soon go home and wait for the Good Lord to take me."

"You will do nothing of the sort, Nanny!" Harry exclaimed. "We need you more than the Lord does, and the Castle would not be home without you."

There was a hint of tears in Nanny's eyes, which made Amorita aware that Harry had said exactly the right thing.

Nanny had always adored Harry.

As Amorita well knew, as far as her Mother and Nanny were concerned, she took second place.

It was her Father who had loved her best of his two children.

Although she did not say so, she missed him desperately.

Now, as she watched Nanny smiling at Harry, she found herself saying a little prayer to her Father.

"Please, help us, Papa," she pleaded. "I know that Harry is reluctant to take me to the Earl of Eldridge's party, and I know you and Mama would be shocked at my pretending to be an actress. But we have to save Nanny, and we must do something about the Castle and all the people who depend upon us. Please . . . please . . . wherever you are . . . help us!"

She had the feeling she had sensed before that her Father heard her and that things would not be as bad as she feared.

She felt a little happier when they left Nanny in the comfortable bedroom.

A pleasant-looking Nurse came in to help her unpack the few things she had brought with her, and get her into bed.

"I will call and see you to-morrow morning," Harry promised as he kissed Nanny good-bye. "Now I am going to see that Amorita goes home."

"That's sensible of you, Master Harry," Nanny replied. "It's not right for Miss Amorita to be wanderin' about London alone."

"Certainly not!" Harry agreed. "So good-bye, Nanny, until to-morrow."

Amorita hugged her old Nurse and said:

"Hurry up and get well, Nanny. You know everything will be in a mess without you."

"I've given Mrs. Briggs instructions which, if she remembers them, will keep everything ticking over until I gets back!" Nanny said firmly.

"And the sooner the better!" Amorita smiled.

She kissed Nanny again, then followed her brother to the door.

She turned as she reached him.

"Good-bye, Nanny," she said. "You know we love you and will be praying that you will be back with us very quickly."

"That's right," Nanny said. "I'll be praying there's not too much of a mess for me to clear up!"

Harry shut the door, and they were both laughing as they went down the stairs.

"Trust Nanny to have the last word!" Harry said. "At the same time, I cannot think how we shall manage without her."

"Everybody will do their best," Amorita said. "At any rate, I will do the cooking for you, and you know I am as good as Mama if I have the right ingredients."

"*If* you have the right ingredients," Harry said. "Those are the operative words, and that is what I must provide, one way or the other."

"And what you *will* provide when you win a race at Elde Castle!" Amorita said.

Harry took her to a Livery Stable.

She had left there the old and rather rickety carriage in which she had come to London.

The horses which drew it were also getting on in years.

They had, however, been trained by Sir Arnold, and Harry knew they would take his sister home safely.

Amorita had driven them herself on the way to

London, and Harry thought now she was tired.

He therefore ordered that Ben, who had come with her, should drive the carriage home.

Ben was an old groom who had been with them for years.

As Harry knew uncomfortably, he had not received proper wages for the last three months.

He was, however, like Nanny, one of the family.

He told Ben they would be going to Elde Castle at the end of the week and he would take part in the races for which the prize money was considerable.

"That'll suit ye, Master 'Arry," Ben said. "On'y trouble be wot ye're goin' to ride."

"That is all settled," Harry answered. "I shall have a choice of His Lordship's finest horses, and I cannot believe I will be stupid enough to pick a loser."

"Don' 'ee dares even think o' it!" Ben said. "As yer Father's son, it'd be a sad day fer all on us if ye don' come in first."

"That is just what I have been saying," Amorita said as she smiled.

She climbed into the carriage, then put her arms around Harry as he placed a rug over her knees.

"Try not to worry," she whispered. "Everything is going to be all right—I feel it in my bones!"

"It would be more of a comfort if I could feel

it in my head!" Harry answered. "I am worried, Amorita, and that is the truth!"

She kissed his cheek.

"Just believe that our luck has changed when we most needed it," she said.

"I will try," Harry promised.

Ben whipped up the horses.

Amorita leaned out of the carriage to wave good-bye to her brother.

As Harry swept off his hat, she was thinking he was the most charming brother any girl could have.

"Everything would be perfect," she thought, "if we only had some money! I am sure that what is happening is a gift from the Gods!"

She sent up another little prayer for help.

Then she told Ben about Nanny, and after that they talked about what wanted doing at the Castle.

At the same time, Amorita was worrying in case she let Harry down.

If his friends discovered that he had broken the Social code of behaviour, they might, as he had said, throw him out of Whites Club.

"I must be very, very careful," she told herself.

* * *

Harry was thinking the same thing as he went back to Chelsea.

Milly was surprised to see him.

She had just returned from driving in the Park in her smart carriage drawn by two horses.

She had stopped in Bond Street to purchase an evening gown.

It had cost more than Harry and Amorita could have spent on food for several months.

Her face lit up when Harry appeared.

She was looking exceedingly smart, he noticed, in a fantastic gown trimmed with rows of lace.

Her bonnet was decorated with six scarlet ostrich feathers.

"I wasn't expecting you," Milly exclaimed.

"I need your help," Harry answered.

A pout twisted Milly's red lips.

"If you're going to try and persuade me to come to the party at Elde Castle," she said, "you can save your breath."

"No, it is not that, Milly," Harry said. "Of course you must not offend the Baron."

He thought, as he spoke, that she would be hard put to find another Protector as rich and so obligingly absent for long periods.

When he had been with Milly and enjoyed the excellent food paid for by the Baron, he had often thought how lucky he was.

Now he felt embarrassed at what he was asking her.

At the same time, he knew she would understand.

"I have found somebody to accompany me to

the Castle," he said somewhat tentatively, "but she needs the right sort of clothes to wear, and that is where I need your help."

Milly stared at him.

"Oh, no, Harry!" she exclaimed. "If you think I'm going to let some woman who's not clever or pretty enough to earn her own, borrow my clothes, you're very much mistaken."

Milly tossed her head as she spoke.

She then walked across the room to take off her feathered bonnet in front of an expensive gold-framed mirror.

This was something Harry had not expected.

"Please, help me, Milly," he begged. "I cannot manage without you."

"Well, you'll have to," Milly replied. "It's bad enough not being able to go to the party, which I'd enjoy, as you know I would, but I'm not decking out some other woman who's taking my place, as you might find her more enjoyable than me!"

To Harry's astonishment, he realised she was jealous.

It was the last thing he had expected.

He had always known that Milly was fond of him.

Also, she looked forward, as he did, to the times when the Baron was not at home.

But it had never occurred to him that she might actually be in love with him.

Now he told himself he had been very stupid and it was something he might have expected.

There were, after all, a number of married women who had, in their husband's absence, looked at him with an undoubted invitation in their eyes.

But he had more or less remained faithful to Milly, simply because he liked her.

What was more, she did not expect him to spend money on flowers and perfume, as a Society woman would expect.

She knew as well as he did that he could not afford to give her anything in the way of money.

Now Harry faced the truth, and after a moment he said:

"All right, Milly, you win! I shall have to tell you the truth."

Milly turned round.

"The truth about what, I'd like to know?" she asked sharply.

"You know perfectly well I cannot afford to pay anyone," Harry said quietly, "and so, because I am desperate, and because our old Nurse has to have an expensive operation, my sister Amorita is coming with me to Elde Castle."

"Your—your *sister*?" Milly gasped. "I don't believe it!"

"It is true," Harry said. "When I left you I was in despair knowing I would have to turn down the invitation."

He paused and then continued:

"Then, when I got to Half Moon Street, my sister was waiting to tell me about Nanny. I explained the situation and she has persuaded me to take her in your place."

"But—you can't do that. Your sister's a Lady!" Milly objected.

"That is exactly what I said to her," Harry answered, "but either I take Amorita, or I stay at home and watch the Castle disintegrating while we die of starvation."

There was such a note of despair in his voice that Milly put her arm round his shoulders and said in a different tone:

"Is this the truth, cross your heart and hope to die?"

"It is the gospel truth," Harry replied, "and apart from anything else, I am trusting you with Amorita's reputation, and mine, in telling you what we are planning to do."

"I realise that," Milly answered, "but I can't imagine what your Mother would say if she knew what you were up to!"

"If only you could have come with me, everything would have been different," Harry said.

"Well, I can't," Milly said. "I've got to think of my own comforts, too, and, as you know, the old boy's very generous."

"You know I would be generous to you if only

I could afford it," Harry said quietly.

"I know that, Silly," Milly said.

She put her hand on his cheek.

"All right. I'll help you," she agreed. "If it comes to that, I'd rather you were taking your sister than some other girl as I'd want to scratch her eyes out!"

"Then you will help me?" Harry asked with a note of triumph in his voice.

"I'll help you," Milly agreed. "I knows exactly the sort of things she'll want, and Lord knows, I've got enough clothes in my wardrobe to last a hundred years. It's time I threw a few out and bought a new trousseau!"

She laughed as she spoke, and Harry asked:

"For the Baron?"

"No, for you, Stupid!" Milly replied.

As she finished speaking, she put her cheek against his and he held her close against him.

Then she said:

"Now, come on—it's a bit early for that! We'd better choose the things that'll make your sister shine even among a possé of Cyprians!"

Harry laughed.

Then they were walking, hand-in-hand, up the stairs towards Milly's bedroom.

chapter three

AMORITA was worried.

It was Thursday. There was no sign of Harry and she did not know what had happened.

All possibilities swept through her mind.

He might have found somebody else to take her place, or he might have given up in despair.

Whatever the reasons, she was concerned that the bill for Nanny's operation was going to be larger than they had at first expected.

She wondered what was to be done about the other servants, whose wages had not been paid for some months.

'We cannot go on like this!' she thought despairingly when she said her prayers.

She liked to feel that her Father and Mother were listening, but her prayers seemed to go unanswered.

She had made the bed and opened the windows in Harry's room to let in the sunshine.

Then, as she was going downstairs, she heard the sound of wheels on the drive.

She ran into the hall as quickly as she could and looked out.

A Phaeton driven by Harry was just drawing up at the front-door.

As the horses came to a standstill, she had run down the steps to him.

"You have come! You have come!" she cried excitedly as he handed the reins to a groom.

"I have come," Harry said, "and I hope you appreciate the conveyance in which I intend to carry you to the Castle to-morrow."

It was certainly very smart, and drawn by two outstanding horses.

"Where did you get it?" Amorita asked nervously.

"Charlie lent it to me," Harry explained. "He said: 'I do not suppose you have anything better than a wheel-barrow in which to take your Cyprian to the party, so I will lend you something more up to scratch.'"

"That was very kind of him," Amorita said as she smiled.

"I thought so too, but I left him guessing as to who was coming with me."

"He will not suspect who it might be?"

Although there was no-one to hear their

conversation, Amorita kept her voice low.

Harry shook his head.

"No, and now you will have to help me bring in the things from the Phaeton, as we have no footmen available."

Amorita laughed.

"It is us, or nobody!"

"I know that," he said, "and I also have Charlie's groom with me. I am trying to impress him."

Amorita looked nervous.

"He is not ... coming with us ... to the Castle?"

"No, of course not," Harry replied. "He is going back in a Post Chaise which Charlie is paying for."

"Lord Raynam has certainly done you proud!" Amorita said with relief.

"He owes me one or two favours," Harry answered in a lofty manner.

He did not explain what they were, and Amorita did not like to ask him.

She had the feeling that they were sinking deeper and deeper into a bottomless pit of lies.

She was, however, thrilled when, from the back of the Phaeton, Harry drew out two trunks and three bonnet boxes.

She looked at them excitedly as they carried them up the steps and into the hall.

Harry went down again to say to the groom:

"Will you take the horses to the stables? They are under that arch."

He pointed in the direction as he spoke, and went on:

"You will find the old groom there, but the rest of the stable lads are out in the fields, training the horses."

This was untrue, but the groom touched his cap respectfully.

Harry watched the horses drive away towards the stables.

He thought enviously what it would mean to him to own such a team.

Then he told himself with a twist of his lips:

'If wishes were horses, beggars would ride.'

He went into the Castle.

Amorita had already opened one of the trunks and was looking at the gowns without taking them out.

"They must have been very expensive, Harry," she said as her brother joined her, "but they are all in rather dashing colours!"

"I know that," Harry agreed, "and they will not really suit you. The person from whom I borrowed them is dark and looks her best in red, emerald green, and a very vivid pink."

Amorita touched the soft satin of one gown and said:

"The colour of my hair doesn't matter, and we do not want anyone to take any notice of me. The only thing I am afraid of is that they might do so if I am wearing these gowns."

"There will be all the other women for them to notice," Harry answered. "You do not want to attract attention. All you must do is to be quiet and ineffectual."

"I think I am that anyway," Amorita said.

She closed the lid of the trunk, saying:

"There is no point in us unpacking anything, because we are taking them to the Castle to-morrow."

"No, I thought of that," Harry agreed, "but you will have to have something decent in which to travel."

Amorita gave a little cry.

"Of course I must! How stupid of me! Oh, Harry, you must take great care of me so that I do not make mistakes."

Harry put his arm round his sister's shoulders.

"You will be all right," he said. "I hope you have found the cosmetics that you had for the Nativity Play. Anyway, Milly told me she had put some in one of the trunks, just in case you do not have the right sort."

"Is that the name of the lady from whom you borrowed all these things?" Amorita asked. "I am very, very grateful to her and I will write and tell her so when you take them back."

"She says you can keep them," Harry replied. "She was going to dispose of them anyway."

"Dispose of them?" Amorita exclaimed. "She must be very rich!"

Harry thought this was a subject to be glossed over, so he said quickly:

"Now, let me see—she did tell me which trunk had the day-gowns in it. I think this is the one."

He picked it up, saying:

"I will carry it upstairs and put it in your room. You bring the bonnet boxes. You will have to choose something to wear on your head."

"Yes, of course," Amorita replied.

They went up the stairs.

Harry put the trunk down on the floor of her bedroom and opened it.

Amorita found the make-up in one of the bonnet boxes.

When she had done so, she started to laugh.

"What is so funny?" Harry asked.

"Just look at these bonnets!" Amorita said. "If I wear those, I will look like a 'cock-a-doodle-do' with all those ostrich feathers!"

"You will look very smart, and very lovely!" Harry said. "That is all that matters!"

"I only hope you will not be disappointed," Amorita said.

But Harry was not listening.

He had gone to his own room, thinking as he did so that it was a terrible mistake to take Amorita to the Castle.

He only hoped she would pass unnoticed.

They must manage to leave as soon as he had won one of the races.

He had a feeling that Saturday night would be the most dangerous time.

Then everyone could drink as much as they wished without feeling they would not do their best on the race-course.

He expected there would also either be dancing to an Orchestra, or gambling.

That meant that the women would take the money that was won, and the Gentlemen would pay for the losses.

That was certainly something he could not afford to do.

If, instead, the girls put on a performance, then that was something in which Amorita could not be included.

"I have to think of every eventuality," Harry told himself. "If we put one foot wrong, we will be unmasked."

He knew, however, that he must not frighten Amorita.

He guessed she would be trying on the gowns to make sure they fitted her.

He thought that she and Milly were almost the same size.

He was therefore not surprised when she came in later to say delightedly:

"Oh, Harry, the gowns fit me perfectly! They are just slightly large in the waist, but if I have time I can alter them, and if not, I will pin them."

"I thought that is what you would do," Harry said.

"You are so very, very clever to have found them for me," Amorita said, "but then, have you ever been anything else?"

"I have not been very clever to have got into the mess we are in now!" Harry said gloomily.

"But we have this opportunity for you to make a lot of money when we least expected it," Amorita said, "and I was desperate about Nanny when I came to London. And, after all, *you* have the solution!"

"Do not 'count your chickens,' " Harry said warningly. "I have not yet won a race!"

"There are four, as it happens."

"Well then, you have four opportunities, and perhaps you will win four-thousand pounds."

"Now, that is being greedy," Harry replied. "I shall be eternally grateful for winning one race. Do not forget, I have some of the best riders in London to compete against—Charlie Raynam, for one."

"As he has been so kind as to lend you a Phaeton, perhaps you will allow him to beat you just once," Amorita said smiling.

She was looking happier, Harry realised, now that she knew the clothes fitted her.

He supposed he should have told her before that she and Milly were the same size.

He had already lain awake at night thinking that they were walking on a tight-rope.

He had stayed on in London because Milly had wanted him to.

He was exceedingly grateful to her for giving Amorita the clothes, also because he felt rather guilty that she loved him.

Quite a number of Gentlemen who had Cyprians under their protection believed they were loved for themselves rather than for what they could afford to spend.

As Harry could give Milly nothing, he was aware that she was really fond of him.

But he had no wish to break her heart.

He had, however, stayed with her because she had asked him to.

As he was leaving, she had put her arms round his neck.

"While you're seeing all those pretty women in a bunch, so to speak," she said, "don't you go forgetting me."

"You know I could never do that," Harry replied. "I am more grateful to you than I can ever say."

"There's no need for words," Milly answered. "And if it comes to that, I'll take your thanks in kisses. They don't cost you anything!"

Harry kissed her.

When he finally left he knew that she was upset at not being able to go with him.

Yet he was quite sure that she would be clever and experienced enough to make the Baron believe she had been counting the days until his return.

"What I must do," Harry told himself as he drove towards his lodgings, "is to marry a rich heiress and settle down."

Then he laughed at the very idea of it.

Any rich heiress would expect to capture a more important title than his.

He was well aware that ambitious Mamas kept their daughters away from him.

He felt, however, uncomfortably guilty when Amorita came down to breakfast next morning wearing the gown in which she was to travel.

It was expensive and elaborate, but very attractive.

It was ornamented with an enormous amount of flounces and was a brilliant blue.

The colour was one that Amorita would never have chosen to wear.

As she came into the Breakfast-Room, Harry exclaimed:

"Oh, you are dressed! That was sensible of you, because I want to leave at about eleven o'clock."

She crossed the room, and as she did so he exclaimed:

"But you are not made up!"

"No," Amorita replied. "I thought I would leave it until the last minute so that it does not get smudged or faded before we get there."

"Oh, for Heaven's sake, take care that does not happen!" Harry exclaimed.

He put down the cup of coffee he was holding in his hand and said:

"Now, listen, Amorita, the Cyp—Actresses—you will meet are all what you—might call 'Professional' women. Apart from acting, they make a business of trying to charm and attract some rich man who will give them the jewellery and other things they require."

He had thought this out during the night.

He felt it was the best way he could describe how the other women would behave.

Amorita looked at him wide-eyed.

"Do you mean that they do not earn enough to keep themselves?" she asked.

"No, of course they do not," Harry said. "Most of them have only small roles, and it is not polite to ask them in what Play they are appearing at the moment, or even what parts they have played."

"I am glad you warned me about that," Amorita said. "What else must I remember?"

"To keep out of sight of the men," Harry said without thinking.

"But, surely, if they have brought one of those ladies with them, they will want to be with her?" Amorita said slowly.

Harry had to think for a moment.

"Yes, yes," he answered, "but there is always a chance that some man will fancy a woman who is with another man."

Amorita was silent.

Then she said:

"What you are saying, Harry, is that you are afraid . . . someone might take . . . a 'fancy' to . . . me."

"Of course I am saying that," Harry agreed. "That is why I want you to stay by me, and talk as little as possible to any man who comes near you."

"That is what I want to do, so it should not be difficult," Amorita replied.

Harry thought that was being over-optimistic.

He just hoped that his friends who had brought their special Cyprians with them would not pay much attention to those of the other men.

However, he was experienced enough to know that a new and pretty face was always of interest to the Bucks and *Beaux* of St. James's Street.

He had heard them often talking about some new Cyprian.

There was always someone to state she was the most outstanding "incomparable" he had ever seen.

This meant some man would be determined to get her into his clutches regardless of to whom she belonged.

It was a conversation in which he had never

joined, for the simple reason that he could not afford to.

Now fragments of it came into his mind, and suddenly he gave a cry.

"What is it?" Amorita asked.

"We have not chosen a name for you!" Harry gasped.

"Do you mean that I cannot use my own?"

"Of course not!" Harry answered. "For one thing, it is too unusual and if, by any chance, Charlie or Jimmy had heard me talk of my sister, they would remember the name 'Amorita.' "

"Of course they would! How clever of you, Harry!" Amorita agreed. "It was stupid of me not to think of that."

"Why should you?" Harry asked gruffly.

"Amorita means 'beloved,' " Amorita said. "Which is what Papa always called Mama, so they gave it as my Christian name."

"I remember," Harry said, "but now let us think what you can be called."

"Oh, please, give me something easy," Amorita begged. "If someone suddenly calls me by a strange name, and I do not reply, they will think it very odd, unless I happen to be stone deaf."

Harry gave a laugh without much humour in it.

"Let me think," he said. "Most actresses use stage names which are not their own."

"What does that mean?" Amorita asked.

"Well, there is one I know called 'Daisy Chain.' She will very probably be at the party."

Amorita laughed.

"That is an amusing name, and, of course, easy to remember."

"That is why she chose it," Harry explained. "Then there is Mavis May, and Barbie Bare."

"That is really funny!" Amorita exclaimed.

"Also," Harry added almost to himself, "Milly Milde."

"I like those names," Amorita said, "and I quite see it is much easier for people to remember those than if they were called Brown, Smith, or Robinson."

"And also much more attractive," Harry agreed.

"Then what am I to be?" Amorita enquired.

There was a pause.

Then Harry said:

"If you were 'Rita,' which is a quite ordinary name, it would be easy to remember it, and why not—'Rita Reele'?"

Amorita clapped her hands.

"That is marvellous! I like that! I shall answer to 'Rita,' and remember that I am really Reele."

"It is doubtful if anyone will ask for your surname," Harry said.

"That makes it even easier," Amorita replied. "You must call me Rita from now on, so that I can get used to it."

She finished what she was eating and got up from the breakfast-table.

"I will go upstairs now and put on my 'war-paint!' " she said. "If I use too much and you are ashamed to be seen with me, you must tell me so."

"I will certainly do that," Harry answered. "I am going to see to my own clothes, and order the Phaeton."

"I have already packed everything you brought with you," Amorita said. "You certainly have some smart evening-clothes!"

"I had to replace the old ones," Harry confessed, feeling somewhat embarrassed. "They were almost in rags!"

"I know," Amorita said. "Mama always liked you to look smart."

She went away without waiting for his answer.

Harry wondered how many other sisters would be so understanding, and so unselfish.

He had not told her that his new evening-clothes were not yet paid for.

That was another bill that would have to be met if he won a race.

"I have to win—I *have* to!" he told himself as he walked towards the stables.

He decided it would be a mistake to eat or drink too much to-night.

He was, like Amorita, thin for his height.

But he found it made him ride lighter, which

was, of course, of importance when he was racing.

Now he thought of it, Amorita was really too thin.

He knew it was so because the meals at the Castle were very sparse.

Also, she had too much to do.

Now he thought that her eyes were almost too big for her small face.

He would not be surprised if every gown he had brought from Millie needed taking in one or two inches round the waist.

"I have to do something about that in the future," he told himself despairingly.

*   *   *

Brother and sister, however, were in good spirits when they set off for Elde Castle.

Harry had lifted the trunks onto the back of the Phaeton.

As he climbed up beside Amorita and took the reins, she asked:

"Are we taking anyone with us?"

"No," Harry said. "Anyway, there is only Ben, and we do not want him talking when he returns."

"I do not think Ben would talk if you told him not to," Amorita said. "At the same time, it is wise not to take any chances."

"There will be servants at the Castle to look

after us," Harry said, "and certainly a maid to look after you."

Amorita laughed.

"I never thought of that. I have always looked after myself."

"But of course there will be one," Harry said. "Be careful what you say to her."

"I think it would be better if I were blind, deaf, and dumb at this party!" Amorita remarked. "Then you would not have to worry about me."

Harry thought he would stop worrying only if she could wear a mask over her face.

He knew, however, it would be a mistake to say so.

He had been astonished when Amorita had appeared dressed in the gown she had worn at breakfast.

He had noticed it showed the curves of her figure, which he had never noticed before.

The bonnet, which matched it, was trimmed with blue ostrich feathers that fluttered with every movement she made.

But what had astonished him more than anything else was her face, now that she was wearing make-up.

She had only lightly touched her eye-lashes with mascara, but he had never realised how long her lashes were or how beautiful her eyes.

Her lips with a touch of pink were a perfect Cupid's bow.

What was more, he had never been aware until then what a straight little aristocratic nose his sister had.

He supposed he was slightly biased.

At the same time, he had to admit she was unquestionably lovely.

It would be difficult for any man, he thought, not to find her enchanting.

They set off, the well-trained horses moving smoothly, and obeying every touch of the reins.

Amorita sat entranced for a while before she said:

"This is thrilling, Harry! It may be difficult once we get there, but I have never been in such a smart carriage before. Nor have I ever been accompanied by such an elegant young man!"

She glanced at her brother as she spoke.

His top-hat was slightly to one side of his head and the points of his collar were high above his chin.

She had washed and pressed his cravat until it was crisp and shiny white.

She saw now that it was tied in a new, intricate fashion.

"Well, at least we have nothing to be ashamed about," Harry said, reassuring himself.

Amorita wanted to add:

"Except for the lies we are telling!"

But she knew it would upset her brother.

Instead, she said:

"I am sure Elde Castle is very impressive. I have often heard it talked about in the past, but I have never met anyone who has been there."

"Until recently, the Earl has been as poor as we are," Harry said.

"Was he really?" Amorita exclaimed. "In that case, if he finds out about us, he will understand."

"He must *not* find out, Amorita!" Harry shouted. "You must understand that no-one else would ever understand that you are not who you are pretending to be."

"I know that," Amorita said soothingly. "Now, stop being upset, Harry, you are spoiling the most exciting thing I have ever been able to do, and that is driving in this lovely Phaeton!"

"I did not mean to shout at you," Harry said apologetically. "However, if you are not nervous—I am!"

"I feel as if a hundred butterflies are fluttering in my breast," Amorita said, "and I have a feeling that if anyone speaks to me, I shall not be able to answer. Apart from that, I keep thinking this is a dream and I shall wake up to find myself in bed!"

"That is a very sensible way to look at it," Harry said approvingly. "Just imagine you are dreaming and none of this is true, then there will be no chance of your being hurt or upset."

"Why should I be?" Amorita asked innocently.

Harry did not reply.

His eyes were on the road ahead.

He was thinking, however, as he had thought before, that they were walking a tight-rope.

They stopped on the way and had luncheon at a Village Inn.

They sat outside in the sunshine and ate freshly-baked bread with a cheese that Amorita said was delicious.

They each drank a glass of homemade cider, then set off again.

It was after four o'clock when they turned in at some wrought-iron gates.

Harry was aware that the long drive was untidy and in need of attention.

He was sure it was going to take some time for the Earl of Eldridge to improve his Estate.

He was even more sure of this when they drove over a bridge which needed repairing.

The court-yard in the front of the Castle lacked gravel and some of the window-panes were cracked.

Harry brought the horses to a standstill on a red carpet, which was obviously new, and ran down the steps.

There were a number of footmen to see to their luggage and a groom to attend to the horses.

The Butler was waiting at the top of the steps to welcome them.

Harry handed his hat and driving-gloves to one of the footmen.

The Butler led them across a large, impressive hall.

As they followed, Harry was aware that the rugs on the floor were almost threadbare.

The portraits of the Earl's ancestors needed cleaning.

Having taken their names, the Butler opened the door of a large Reception-Room and in a stentorian voice announced:

"Sir Edward Howe, M'Lord, and Miss Rita Reele!"

For a moment, because she was nervous, Amorita felt that the room swam in front of her eyes.

She was, however, aware of crystal chandeliers overhead and elegant French furniture.

There was a profusion of flowers everywhere.

From a group of people at one end of the room emerged a tall, handsome man who came towards them.

"I hoped you would get here early, Harry!" the Earl said. "It will give me time to show you the new horses before dinner."

The Earl shook Harry's hand, then looked towards Amorita.

"I do not think you have met Rita Reele," Harry said.

Amorita dropped a small curtsy as the Earl took her hand, saying:

"I am delighted to meet you, and it is very

kind of you to come with my friend Harry."

"It was very kind of you to have me, My Lord," Amorita replied.

She spoke in her usual soft, sweet voice.

Harry thought a little nervously that the Earl seemed surprised.

"Come and meet the others," he said.

He walked back towards the group at the end of the room.

Jimmy and Charlie greeted Harry first.

The Honorable James Ponsonby had with him Mavis, who was dressed from head to toe in scarlet.

Lord Charles Raynam had a Cyprian with him whom Harry knew as Lou-Lou.

To Amorita's surprise, he kissed her affectionately on both cheeks.

"I might have known I'd find *you* here," Mavis remarked, "and if you win all the races, I'll knock your block off!"

She spoke with a slightly Cockney accent.

But she was, Amorita admitted, the most sensual-looking woman she had ever seen.

The other guest was Sir Mortimer Martin.

As he shook hands with Amorita, he looked at her in a piercing manner which she did not like and did not understand.

The woman with him had red hair and green eyes.

She was a Siren-like beauty who certainly was different from most women.

She was called Zena, and there was something in the way she moved which reminded Amorita of a snake.

"I cannot think," Sir Mortimer said as she was staring at Zena, "why I have never met you before."

"I do not know many people," Amorita replied.

"Then, of course," Sir Mortimer replied, "we must make up for lost time."

Because she did not like the way he was talking to her or the look in his eyes, Amorita moved a little closer to Harry.

The Earl was telling him about some new horses which had come down from London yesterday.

"They are first class, Harry!" he was saying. "Charlie got them for me from Montepart, and I am certain there is one amongst them you will want to ride."

"Shall we go and look at them now?" Harry asked eagerly.

"Why not?" the Earl answered. "We have time before tea, and I do not suppose anybody else will want to accompany us."

Amorita was suddenly aware that Harry had forgotten her.

She reached out and touched his arm.

"Oh, Roydin, if you do not mind, I would like to bring Rita with me. She knows a great deal about horses."

There was just a pause before the Earl answered:

"Yes, of course, if she wants to come."

It was obviously something he had not intended, and Amorita felt embarrassed.

At the same time, she had no wish to be left alone with the Earl's other guests.

Sir Mortimer noticed what was happening, and Lou-Lou who was beside him shouted:

"Look 'ere, Roydin, don't you be gone for long, or I'll feel neglected."

The Earl turned to smile at her.

"I will be back almost before you realise I have left," he promised, "but there is a horse which I want Harry to see."

"Well, that's all right, then, as long as it's a horse you're interested in and not a female!" Lou-Lou replied. "I'm not letting you off the leash!"

There was laughter at this.

Amorita thought there was no doubt from the way Lou-Lou spoke that she was not a Lady.

She was thankful that she was leaving the room with Harry.

As she hurried behind them, she became aware that Sir Mortimer was beside her.

"I shall be counting the minutes until you

return," he said in a low voice that only she could hear.

She looked at him in surprise.

Then, seeing the expression in his eyes, she almost ran towards Harry who, with the Earl, had reached the door.

As they crossed the hall, the Earl was talking enthusiastically about the horses he had just bought.

Amorita was asking herself why she should be frightened.

Foolish and unreasonable though it seemed, she knew she was.

chapter four

THEY reached the stables, which were old-fashioned but large enough to house a great number of horses.

"I am longing for you to see the ones that came yesterday," the Earl said to Harry as they walked over the cobblestones.

"I thought Charlie would do you proud," Harry said. "He really knows more than anyone else."

"I think you are being modest," the Earl said, "I would trust your judgement anywhere."

Amorita found herself warming to the way he was speaking, and she knew that Harry was delighted.

They went inside the first stable door.

When she saw what the stalls contained, Amorita knew the Earl had not been exaggerating.

Going from stall to stall, Amorita thought that each one was more magnificent than the last.

As the Earl and Harry discussed them, she kept silent.

She was making a fuss over one very spirited horse, when she was aware that the Earl was watching her.

Because she thought she should make some comment, she said:

"He is very beautiful and full of 'go,' but it is because he is happy, not out of naughtiness."

The Earl laughed and said:

"I can see you love horses, Rita."

Amorita was surprised at the use of her Christian name when he was speaking to her almost for the first time.

Then she thought it probably happened to all the other women and she must appear not to have noticed.

"Horses usually behave well with me," she said simply, "because they know I love them."

The horse was certainly more docile than when she had entered his stall.

The Earl, after watching her for a few minutes, said:

"I suppose what you are really saying is that you would like to ride *Hussar*?"

Amorita realised that was the horse's name.

She turned towards the Earl with her eyes shining.

"Could I really do that?" she asked. "It would be absolutely wonderful if I could!"

"Of course you can," the Earl said, "and now I think about it, I had better have a Ladies' Race. What do you think, Harry?"

Harry, who had moved away to see which horse he wished to ride himself, had not been listening to the conversation.

Now, picking up the last words, he said:

"A Ladies' Race? Yes, a good idea!"

"And, of course, Rita wishes to enter for it," the Earl went on.

Watching her brother, Amorita was not certain if he was surprised or annoyed.

He only remarked:

"She rides very well."

Amorita looked at the Earl.

"Then, please, please, can I ride *Hussar*?"

"You are quite certain he will not be too much for you?" the Earl asked. "He is being quiet at the moment, but I am told the stable-boys are frightened of him."

"I am not," Amorita said, "and my Father always told me that if a horse knows you are frightened, he will play up, just to show his superiority."

"So your Father is a good judge of horse-flesh!" the Earl remarked. "What does he do?"

Amorita was about to answer, when she remembered that this was something she had not discussed with Harry.

It would be a great mistake to invent a Father without his approval.

Without the Earl being aware of it, she touched *Hussar* a little sharply and he immediately reared up.

"Gently, gently, boy!" Amorita said. "You must not behave like that, or they will not let me ride you, and that is something I really want to do."

She was talking in a soft, caressing tone which she believed the horses she had ridden understood.

Only when *Hussar* was quiet again did she turn towards the Earl to say:

"I think if you let me ride *Hussar*, I should feel it was as exciting as if I were flying to the moon!"

"Then he shall be kept for you," the Earl said.

Amorita smiled at him.

"You are very kind."

"I am sure you must find a great number of men," the Earl answered, "who wish to be that where you are concerned."

As if he thought it was a mistake for her to talk to the Earl for too long, Harry called to her.

"Come here, Rita!" he said. "I want you to look at this horse. I feel sure he is a winner."

Hurriedly, because she thought Harry might

disapprove of what she had arranged with the Earl, Amorita ran to the stall.

It certainly contained a very large and strong-looking stallion.

"What do you think?" Harry asked as she inspected him.

"He looks capable of running from here to the North Pole!" Amorita said.

"What I want him to do," Harry said, "is to be first on the race-course."

They were talking to each other in low voices while the Earl was speaking to one of the grooms.

"Then you think I should choose this one?" Harry said.

"I think you know instinctively within yourself if he will suit you or not," Amorita replied. "I knew the moment I saw *Hussar*, that he meant something to me. I cannot explain it, but the feeling was there."

Harry smiled at her.

"And I feel the same about *Crusader*."

"Then you will win," Amorita said.

Harry crossed his fingers and held them up.

She smiled and said:

"Confidence is half the battle! Papa used to say that."

"I know," Harry said, "but he was a better rider than I am."

"Nonsense!" Amorita replied. "You were not

as good as he was because you were younger, but now I think he would be very proud of you."

She knew as she spoke that she had said the right thing.

She was intelligent enough to realise that Harry now needed encouraging.

After all the trouble over money and being unfortunate with one or two horses he had broken in, he was unsure of himself.

She knew she was right in trying to give him confidence.

As the Earl joined them, Harry said:

"This is the horse I would like to ride, Roydin, in the big race, whichever it is."

"That is the first," the Earl replied. "After that it is up to you how many more you enter."

Harry drew in his breath.

Then he said:

"In which case, I had better choose another horse."

"Choose four," the Earl said. "There are plenty available and, as I am not competing, you can keep four without anyone being aware of it."

"I must not be greedy," Harry answered. "I will take two of your best."

Amorita looked at her brother in surprise.

Then she knew without Harry telling her that he did not wish to "steal a march" on his other friends.

After some consideration, they found another horse who was called *Mercury* which both she and Harry thought outstanding.

Then the Earl said that he ought to return to the Castle, as more of his friends would be arriving.

As they walked back he said:

"I want your advice, Harry, when you have time, on modernising the stables. As you have a Castle yourself, you can tell me what repairs and innovations should be put in hand immediately."

"I would love to do that," Harry said, "and I only wish I could do the same to my Castle, although it is very small compared to yours."

"I will come over and see it as soon as I have time," the Earl said.

As he spoke, Amorita flashed a quick glance at Harry.

She was aware that he, too, knew this was something that could not happen.

With what she thought was very quick thinking, he laughed and said:

"Of course! You are welcome at any time, but first things first. Now that you can afford it, you must make your Castle the most outstanding in the whole country."

"I will certainly make it more comfortable than Windsor Castle," the Earl said. "I stayed there last year. My bed was as hard as a board and I lost myself every night in the corridors before I could find my own bedroom."

Harry laughed.

"A great many people have made that excuse for obvious reasons!"

"Well, mine, believe it or not," the Earl said firmly, "was because I was tired and wanted to sleep."

The two men laughed as if he had said something funny.

Amorita wondered vaguely what they were talking about.

She was looking round her, thinking that the garden wanted a great deal done to it before it was as perfect as it should be.

She could also see quite clearly what needed to be done to the outside of the Castle itself.

When they went back into the Drawing-Room, it was to find that a number of other guests had arrived.

The women who accompanied the men looked even more spectacular than those Amorita had met already.

In fact, the gowns were elaborate enough for the Stage and their bonnets fantastic.

Amorita thought her Mother would have been horrified at anyone looking so overdressed in the country.

Tea was served, and she was impressed by the George III silver tea-pot and kettle on a large silver tray.

She suspected that it was all entailed like their own silver.

The Earl, like Harry, had therefore been unable to sell it to pay his bills.

"I suppose," she told herself, "he was very lucky that he could not dispose of it. If he had done so and now come into the fortune, he would bitterly regret the treasures that had been taken from the Castle."

She must have been looking serious while she was saying this.

To her consternation, Sir Mortimer, who had been at the other end of the room, came to her side.

"Why are you not smiling with those sweet lips which were made for kisses?" he asked.

For a moment Amorita looked at him in astonishment.

No-one had ever spoken to her like that before.

She was not certain whether she should ignore it, or tell Sir Mortimer not to be familiar.

"I cannot understand," he said before she could speak, "why I have not seen you in London. Has Harry kept you locked up so that you cannot be stolen from him?"

"I have been in the country," Amorita managed to say rather coldly.

"That accounts for it," Sir Mortimer said. "But now that we have met, when I go back to London I shall find you, even if you try to hide from me."

Because Amorita felt as if it was a threat, she moved away from him.

Harry was standing talking to Jimmy Ponsonby.

As he realised she was beside him, he said:

"Oh, Jimmy, I do not think you have met Rita."

"No," Jimmy replied, "and I am enchanted to do so."

He shook hands with Amorita, and said:

"Have you known Harry for long? If you have, it is extremely mean of him not to have let us meet before."

"I have been in the country," Amorita said demurely for the second time.

"Ah, that accounts for it," Jimmy said, "but you do not look very countrified to me."

He glanced at her hat with its blue feathers as he spoke.

Amorita wanted to laugh.

It was obvious, she told herself, that fine feathers made people treat her in a very different way from how they had ever done before.

As if Harry were aware of this, he said:

"I expect after our long drive you would like to lie down before dinner."

"Yes, of course I would," Amorita said obediently.

"Then I will take you to the Housekeeper," Harry said, "who will show you to your room."

They were walking towards the door, when the Earl saw them and said:

"Just a minute, Harry. I want to tell everyone what I have planned."

Harry and Amorita stood waiting, and he said:

"Now you are all here, except for two people who are coming on later, I have planned that to-night we have dinner and go to bed comparatively early, so that you will be at your best to-morrow when we start racing at eleven o'clock."

Everyone was listening intently, and he went on:

"There will be two races before Luncheon and two after, with an additional one, which will be a Ladies' Race."

There was a shriek from some of the women at this, and one of them near to Amorita exclaimed:

"I hope to God I've remembered to bring a riding-habit with me!"

As she spoke, Amorita looked desperately at Harry.

She did not need to ask the question aloud, and he said in a low voice:

"Do not worry. I am sure Milly has thought of it. She rides herself."

Amorita gave a little sigh of relief.

The Earl continued:

"When all the hard work is over, we will really enjoy ourselves. I have arranged a stage to be erected in the Ball-Room, and the girls will parade in front of us while we have a secret vote on who we make the winner."

"A *secret* vote?" one man exclaimed.

"Of course," the Earl replied, "otherwise you, Henry, with your roving eye, might find yourself in trouble."

There was a shriek of laughter at this, and the Earl went on:

"The first Incomparable will win the same as the prizes for the races, and just so that there will be no hard feelings, there will be a souvenir for everyone who enters."

There was a murmur of delight at this.

One woman put her arms round the Earl's neck and kissed him on the cheek.

"I'm delighted you're so rich, Roydin!" she said. "And I'm out to enjoy every penny of it!"

There was more laughter and a great number of witty remarks.

Then Harry took Amorita's arm and drew her quickly to the door.

When he got outside, he said:

"Do not worry. I am sure Milly will have put a riding-habit in for you. If not, ask the Housekeeper for help. The Castle is certain to have a whole collection of things in the attic, rather like we have at home."

"If I cannot ride *Hussar*, I shall cry my eyes out!" Amorita said.

"You will receive a lot of compliments if you do," Harry said.

He spoke somewhat cynically.

Because Amorita thought he was referring to Sir Mortimer, she said:

"Try to stop that man from talking to me. There is something unpleasant about him, and his compliments are really rather rude."

"Keep away from him," Harry said. "He should not be here in the first place. Papa would say he was a complete bounder!"

"I certainly do not encourage him," Amorita said. "And do make sure that I am not seated next to him at dinner."

Harry nodded.

"I will do that."

They reached the bottom of the stairs.

As Harry looked up, he saw, as he expected, that the Housekeeper was standing on the first landing.

"There she is," he said in a low voice to Amorita. "Be pleasant to her and do not be upset if she is rather stiff and offhand."

Amorita was surprised, but she did not say anything.

She merely climbed the stairs while Harry went back to the Drawing-Room.

He was thinking as he did so that it was always the servants on these occasions who resented having to wait on Cyprians.

In their own parlance, they thought of them as "no better than they should be."

He remembered long ago he had gone to the same sort of party given by one of his friends.

One of the Cyprians had complained to him how offensive the servants were.

"They give themselves such airs," she said, "that you'd think we'd come out of the gutter! It's the last time I ever stay in a country house if I can help it. I prefers a Hotel, where they looks after you whoever you are."

Knowing how snobby most senior servants were, Harry had not been surprised.

Now he thought that he should have warned Amorita before that this was something she might encounter.

At the same time, it was increasingly difficult to explain to her why these things should happen to someone who was supposed to be an actress.

"If I win to-morrow," he told himself, "we will go home. I am certain Amorita will not wish to parade herself in the Ball-Room."

Upstairs, the Housekeeper, rustling in black silk with the chatelaine at her waist, said:

"Good-evening, Miss! If you'll tell me your name, I'll take you to the room in which you're sleeping."

"Thank you," Amorita said. "I am Rita Reele,

and do tell me what you are called."

"I'm Mrs. Dawson," the Housekeeper replied. "Please come this way."

She walked ahead, moving, Amorita thought, with her head stiff as if she were performing an unpleasant duty.

She opened the door of a room.

It was large and very attractive, although the wall-paper was peeling in one corner.

The curtains were faded and the carpet worn in several places.

At the same time, the huge four-poster with its exquisite carving and embroidered curtains made Amorita look at it with delight.

"What a pretty room!" she exclaimed. "The carving is wonderful!"

She was looking as she spoke at the dressing-table.

An oval mirror had gilt Cherubs on either side of it.

There was a looking-glass over the mantel-piece of the same period.

Without thinking, Amorita said:

"That is beautiful and very like one we have at home, which I should think is of the same period."

The Housekeeper looked at her in surprise.

Amorita was aware that at the far end of the room her trunks were being unpacked by two maids wearing mob-caps.

"How kind of you to unpack for me," she said. "Please, will you look and see if there is a riding-habit?"

"A riding-habit?" the Housekeeper exclaimed. "I think, Miss, you'll find the horses in the stables very different from those that trit-trot in the Park."

She spoke in a manner as if she were "taking down a peg or two" an uppish School-girl.

Amorita smiled:

"His Lordship has already let me choose one I can ride that is very spirited, but I am sure I can handle him."

She saw the doubt in the Housekeeper's face, and added:

"I live in the country, so as it happens, I have never 'trit-trotted' in the Park, and have no desire to do so."

"If you live in the country, Miss," the Housekeeper answered tartly, "I can't believe you'd have much use for the sort of gowns the maids are putting in the wardrobe."

As she spoke, one of the maids in question drew out one that was of a brilliant, fiery pink.

It was festooned round the hem with feathers dyed in the same colour.

Amorita laughed.

Because it seemed so ridiculous after what she had said, she explained:

"These clothes are not mine. I borrowed them

for the very auspicious occasion of staying in this magnificent Castle."

The Housekeeper looked at her as if to ask if she was telling the truth.

Then she said:

"In that case, Miss, I think the colours are wrong for you."

"I thought that myself," Amorita said in a confiding manner. "At the same time, one should not 'look a gift-horse in the mouth!' "

The Housekeeper actually laughed.

"That's true enough, and something I've always thought myself when times was bad."

Amorita looked at her sympathetically.

"I know you have had a hard time here," she said, "and it must be very exciting for you that His Lordship has come into a fortune."

"We can hardly believe it, Miss, and that's the truth!" Mrs. Dawson said. "We're hoping now things will go back to how they were in the old days when I were a young girl and went into service to help my family."

"Then I am very, very glad that things have changed," Amorita replied, "and the Castle will soon be as magnificent as it must have been originally."

She spoke with such sympathy that the stiffness and disdain seemed swept away from Mrs. Dawson's face.

"Now, you let me help you undress, Miss,"

she said, "and have a nice rest before dinner. If you've come a long way to get here, you must be tired."

"I am a little," Amorita admitted.

She had not slept at all well the previous night for worrying.

The Housekeeper helped her into bed.

The maids had finished unpacking and the curtains were drawn to shut out the light.

"I'll have you called," Mrs. Dawson promised, "in plenty of time before dinner, and I expect you'd like a bath."

"I would love one," Amorita answered, "if it is not too much trouble."

"It'll be no trouble," Mrs. Dawson said, "and I'll bring you some of my special perfume to use in it."

"Oh, thank you," Amorita replied. "When my Mother was alive, she used to distill violets in the Spring. But now she is dead, I have been too busy."

"I'll bring you some violet oil, if I still have it by me," Mrs. Dawson promised. "Now shut your eyes and rest, Miss. It's doubtful, whatever His Lordship says, that you'll get early to bed."

"Oh, I do hope I can," Amorita answered. "I want to feel my best when I am riding to-morrow."

"Then you'll just have to creep away," Mrs. Dawson said. "I knows what these evenings are like. Too much drink, too much noise, and everyone paying for it the next day!"

She did not wait for an answer, but went out of the room, shutting the door.

Amorita thought she must warn Harry.

Neither of them could afford to "pay for it" the following day when there were races to be won.

Everything depended on Harry being the winner.

'Perhaps I too could win a prize,' Amorita thought, 'and that would be wonderful, wonderful! I might even be able to pay for Nanny myself instead of taking the money from the Castle.'

This was such a comforting thought that she snuggled down against the pillows and shut her eyes.

* * *

It seemed a long time later that she heard the door open and thought it was Mrs. Dawson coming to call her.

Then she heard Harry ask:

"Are you awake, Amorita?"

"Oh, it is you, Harry!" Amorita replied, sitting up in bed. "What is happening?"

"I have come up to dress for dinner," Harry said. "I suppose you know I am next door?"

It was then Amorita realised he had come in through a door which she had not noticed.

"You are next door?" she exclaimed. "How

splendid! I am so glad. It was kind of the Earl to put us together."

Harry wondered how he could explain that it was something a host would obviously do, seeing who he thought she was.

Instead, he pulled back the curtains to let in the light and walked to the bed, saying:

"You are certainly comfortable here!"

"It is lovely, is it not?" Amorita said. "And I have this huge bed all to myself. I have been thinking how lucky I am."

Harry sat down.

"Now, listen, Amorita," he said. "You must try and slip away soon after dinner because neither of us wants to be tired when we are riding to-morrow."

"I thought you would say that. Mrs. Dawson was frightening me by saying everybody would be very late going to bed, and would drink too much. That is something you must not do."

"It is something I have no intention of doing," Harry said, "but it may be difficult to get away, unless we are clever about it."

"Then what are we to do?" Amorita asked.

"Just slip out of the room without anyone being aware of it," Harry said.

He paused, and she thought he was trying to find words in which to explain something.

"What is it, Harry?" she asked. "What is wrong?"

"I am just worrying about what you will think of to-night," he said. "Some people do drink a lot, then they behave in a way one would not expect."

Amorita looked puzzled, and he said:

"What I am saying is—try not to listen to the stupid things men say to you, and do not gossip with the women."

"I do not want to," Amorita replied. "I am so frightened of saying something wrong that I really want only to talk to you."

"That is exactly what we must try to arrange," Harry said. "I have already spoken to Roydin, and told him that you want to sit next to me at dinner, and not be anywhere near Sir Mortimer."

"Did you say that to him?" Amorita said. "I hope he will not repeat it to Sir Mortimer, but I think he is a horrid man, and I shall try to avoid him."

"You do that," Harry said, "and we will slip away as early as we can. Nobody will really think it strange."

"Why not?" Amorita asked.

This was a question Harry had no intention of answering, so he rose to his feet.

"I am going to dress now," he said. "I expect a maid will be coming to attend to you."

"I hope so," Amorita replied. "I have been promised a bath, and one that is scented, too!"

"You are being spoiled!" Harry said. "At the

same time, Amorita, you deserve it. You know I am grateful, very, very grateful, and I have no right to bring you to this party."

"Do be careful what you say," Amorita warned.

"Do not worry," Harry said. "I am so careful, I am watching every word I utter like a hawk!"

Amorita laughed as he went out by the door through which he had entered the room and shut it behind him.

"I cannot think," Amorita said to herself, "why he worries so much. Everything is really going very smoothly so far."

She was thinking of *Hussar* as she spoke, knowing that any difficulties were unimportant beside the fact that she could ride that magnificent horse.

chapter five

AMORITA found herself sitting at dinner next to Harry and Charles Raynam.

They continually talked about horses, across her, and she enjoyed every word of it.

She was, however, aware that the other women were behaving in a most extraordinary way.

They talked seductively to the men next to them as if they were alone, also continually touched them with their hands or even, towards the end of the meal, kissed them.

There was no doubt, however, that everybody was enjoying themselves, because the noise and laughter grew louder and louder.

Once or twice, because it was so extraordinary, Amorita looked at Harry as if to ask him what it was all about.

At last, after five excellent courses, the meal finished.

Amorita knew it was time for the ladies to leave the gentlemen to their port, but there was no sign of them doing so.

As if he read her thoughts, the Earl asked in a loud voice:

"Are you girls going to retire, or are you waiting for us to come with you?"

"You don't suppose we're going to leave you alone to get into mischief, do you?" Zena asked.

"Or to drink too much port!" another elaborately dressed Cyprian chimed in.

"Very well," the Earl said. "I think it is a mistake before the races for us men to drink too much. So we will come with you into the Drawing-Room."

There were shrieks of delight at this.

Molly, the girl sitting on the Earl's right, flung her arms around him and kissed him on the lips.

Amorita stared in astonishment.

Then Harry nudged her.

"Take no notice," he whispered.

She thought she had made a *faux pas*, and rose to leave with Harry walking beside her.

As they reached the corridor, he said:

"If you want to go to bed, this is your chance, but make it look as if we are going into the garden."

Amorita wanted to ask why, but he took her

by the arm and drew her out by a side door.

She was aware as they did so that Charles was following.

He had with him a very attractive woman who had sat on his other side at dinner.

To Amorita's delight, there was a fountain playing in the centre of the lawn.

"Oh, a fountain!" she exclaimed. "I have always wanted to have one at home."

"You can see it another time," Harry said.

He took her round the corner of the house, and when they were out of sight of Charles, he said:

"You can see it is going to be rowdy. You go up to bed. I do not want anyone making comments about you."

"Why should they?" Amorita asked innocently.

Harry did not reply.

He merely found another door into the Castle, which fortunately was open, and they went up a side staircase to their floor.

"Now go to bed and go to sleep," he said as they reached Amorita's bedroom.

"You are not going down again," she asked quickly.

"No, of course not," he said. "They will think we have left together."

Amorita did not understand, but she was glad that Harry was not going to drink any more.

She had thought quite a number of men and women at dinner were flushed in the face and being noisy because they had drunk too much.

"Mama would be horrified!" she told herself.

She shut the door of her bedroom.

She heard Harry moving about next door and was just going to ask him to undo her gown.

Then Mrs. Dawson knocked on the door and came in.

"I expect you'd like me to help you undress, Miss," she said.

"That is kind of you," Amorita answered. "I usually manage by myself, but this gown is rather complicated."

Mrs. Dawson did not reply.

She unbuttoned Amorita's gown and hung it up in the wardrobe.

Then she said:

"What time would you like to be called in the morning, Miss?"

"Oh, early, please," Amorita said. "I want to have a chance of looking at the horses again before the races, so could you please make it seven o'clock."

Mrs. Dawson raised her eye-brow.

"That's very early, Miss. You're quite certain you don't want to rest for longer?"

"Oh, no," Amorita replied. "I usually get up earlier than that."

Mrs. Dawson seemed about to say something.

Instead, she went to the door.

"Good-night, Miss," she said, "and I *hope* you sleep well."

There was a strange note in her voice, which made Amorita wonder what she meant.

Then, because she was really tired, she blew out the lights and got into bed.

She could still hear Harry in the next room, then there was silence.

She thought with relief that he would get a good night's sleep, which was essential if he was to win to-morrow.

"Please . . . God . . . please let . . . him win," she prayed.

Amorita awoke with a start and realised that her curtains were being pulled back.

She knew it must be seven o'clock and sat up in bed.

The maid came from the window, saying:

"Mrs. Dawson says, Miss, you're t'be called at seven, but there be nobody at breakfast afore eight."

"I want to go to the stables," Amorita answered.

She dressed quickly.

Only as she washed and started to dress did she remember she had not yet seen the riding-habit Milly had sent for her.

As the maid brought it from the wardrobe, she

realised that it was what she imagined was worn in the Park.

It was not at all the sort of habit of which her Father would have approved for riding in the country.

There was, however, nothing she could do about it.

She had to admit that the bright blue of the skirt and jacket and the elaborate lace blouse were becoming, if unsuitable.

The maid found in a bonnet box the riding-hat to go with it.

She was just about to leave the bedroom, when she remembered she had not made up her face.

She thought Harry would be angry if she appeared without her paint and powder, and quickly put it on.

Then, because she thought she was wasting time, she ran down the stairs and out towards the stables.

She was not surprised when she got there to find that Harry was already in the stall with *Crusader*.

He looked round as Amorita joined him, and said:

"You are early!"

"I wanted to look at these horses again," Amorita said, "and I guessed you might be here."

"If I cannot win on *Crusader*, I will never win

on anything!" Harry said.

"Of course you will win," Amorita replied.

Harry glanced over his shoulder, then he said in a low voice:

"Make sure you are standing near me if I receive a prize, and I will give it to you at once."

He spoke so surreptitiously that Amorita asked:

"Why is that important?"

Harry hesitated for a moment. Then he said:

"On occasions like this, the winner often gives what he has won to a woman, and sometimes if he does not do so, she takes it."

Amorita gasped:

"Do you mean . . . if I am not there . . . someone else might . . . take it from . . . you?"

Harry nodded.

"You can understand that if they do so, it would be difficult to insist on having it back."

Amorita gave a cry:

"Oh, Harry, I am glad you told me. You must give it to me at once. You know we need every penny of it!"

"Exactly!" Harry agreed.

Amorita wondered where she could put it.

She undid the front of her jacket and found, as she suspected, there was an inside pocket.

'I will put it in there,' she thought, 'then button up my coat again.'

The idea of somebody else taking Harry's winnings away was horrifying.

If he did not win any other money, it would be that which would save Nanny's life.

They looked at some of the other horses, then walked back to the Castle.

"I shall be praying all the time you are riding," Amorita said.

"Thank you," Harry replied. "You know without my saying so that I would not be here if it had not been for you."

They smiled at each other, then went into the Breakfast-Room.

The Earl was already there, so were four other men, but there was no sign of the women.

"I need not ask where you have been," the Earl said, rising to his feet as Amorita and Harry came into the room.

"I was just making sure that *Crusader* had not been spirited away in the night," Harry said, "or stolen by robbers."

The Earl laughed.

"I can think of other things they might take first."

"I personally would rather have the treasures out of the stable than those in the Castle," Charles said.

"It depends," Jimmy laughed, "if they are walking on four or two legs."

"This morning and this afternoon we will concentrate on the horses," the Earl said, "but after last night, I have different plans for the evening."

Those sitting round the table were listening.

Two other men, one of them being Sir Mortimer, who had just come into the room, stopped talking.

"What I thought we would do," the Earl said, "is to have the parade to choose the most beautiful 'Incomparable' before dinner."

"What you are implying," Jimmy said jokingly, "is that we might be too drunk afterwards to put our vote in the right place!"

"That did cross my mind," the Earl said, "but I think also that the ladies will look at their best when they first leave their bedrooms. If after dinner they feel like entertaining us, that will be a different matter."

"Personally," Charles said, "I think that is very sensible."

"I thought you would agree," the Earl said as he smiled, "so we will vote at seven-thirty, have dinner at nine, then the fun can go on indefinitely into the night."

"I think that is an excellent idea," Sir Mortimer said, "and, as you say, we want to be at our best when we are voting who is the most beautiful woman present."

Before anyone could answer, the door opened

and Zena came in accompanied by two other women.

They were all dressed in extremely glamorous gowns.

Then Zena looked at Amorita and exclaimed:

"Are you going in for the Ladies' Race? I've never imagined you on horseback."

"I have ridden a great deal in my life," Amorita said quietly.

"Well, if you come in last," Zena said in an unpleasant voice, "I dare say His Lordship'll have a consolation prize for you."

She turned away as she spoke to inspect the food that was arranged on the sideboard.

Harry said in a low voice:

"Do not answer her. She is a good rider, and determined to win."

Amorita pressed her lips together.

She thought if only she could win the Ladies' Race she could pay for Nanny's operation and the overdue wages for Briggs.

That would leave Harry's money for the repairs to the Castle.

The rest of the party came down to breakfast in "dribs and drabs."

Soon after ten o'clock the Earl and Charles said they were going to the race-course.

"Are you coming with us, Harry?" the Earl asked.

"Yes, of course," Harry answered.

Frightened of being left out of it, Amorita ran upstairs to collect her gloves.

As she came down again, Harry was waiting for her in the hall, but the other men had gone on ahead.

"I am sorry if I delayed you," Amorita said.

"Roydin thought it was strange that you should want to come with us," Harry explained, "rather than travel in the carriages with the other women. But I thought you would hate it."

"It is only Zena," Amorita said. "The others are quite pleasant."

"She is a nasty piece of work, like Sir Mortimer," Harry said. "Watch out when you are riding that she does not deliberately get in your way."

"I thought that myself," Amorita said, "but she is determined that I cannot ride, so I expect she will ignore me."

"I think Roydin will see there is no bumping and boring," Harry said. "He is not competing, but just keeping a strict eye on everybody."

Amorita thought that was a good thing.

When they reached the race-course, it was to find that the horses were already there, and the Earl was mounted.

As she looked at him, Amorita thought she might have known that he would be an outstanding rider.

Her Father had always said that a man should look part of the horse he was riding.

That was certainly true of the Earl.

He was mounted on a magnificent black stallion with Arab blood in him.

Amorita found it hard to keep her eyes off the Earl.

He was organising everything in a way which she knew was brilliant.

He deserved the appreciation of Harry and the other men.

When the race started, she saw Harry move into place on *Crusader*.

She sent up a special prayer that he would be the winner.

There was no doubt that he was riding the best horse in the race.

The Earl started them and they had to go three times round the race-course.

The third time round he was waiting at the winning-post, and Amorita walked across the grass to stand beside him.

In a voice that only she could hear, he bent down towards her and said:

"I think Harry will do it."

"I am praying that he will," Amorita answered.

"I thought that was what you were doing," the Earl remarked.

The horses came nearer, and now she could see that Harry was in front of the other riders.

They were trying by every means in their power to overtake him.

He passed the winning-post half a length ahead.

"Bravo!" the Earl cried. "Well done!"

Amorita could not speak.

She felt as if she must cry from sheer happiness that Harry had been successful.

The riders pulled in their horses, then came back to where the grooms were waiting.

They were all congratulating Harry.

Then they walked to where the Earl was now standing, on a small platform, with a table in front of him.

Surrounding him were the women looking like a bunch of brilliant flowers.

There was also quite a crowd of onlookers.

It comprised those who were working on the Estate and those who had come up from the village.

Harry knew, although he had not said anything to Amorita, that the Earl had deliberately not asked any of his County neighbours to the races.

Now, as the last rider came up to the table, the Earl said:

"Well done, Harry! You rode magnificently and certainly deserve your prize."

He handed him a cheque as he spoke, which Amorita could see was made out for a thousand pounds.

Harry swept off his hat and bowed as he took it from the Earl.

Then, as several women moved forward as if to embrace him, Amorita was there first.

She put one arm round Harry and kissed his cheek.

As she did so, she felt him press the cheque into her hand.

She slipped it quickly into the pocket of her jacket, which she had undone.

She was only just in time.

As she took her arms from around his neck, Zena was there, saying in her seductive tones:

"Congratulations, dear Harry! I'm sure you'll share your winnings with those who love you!"

"I have done that already," Harry said bluntly, and moved away from her.

The next race, which was slightly delayed, found Harry riding one of the horses that had been brought down from the stables.

The race was won by Charles, Jimmy was second, and there were three contestants for third place.

For one moment it did not seem possible to put a pin between them.

Then at the last fifty yards, Harry managed, Amorita thought, by almost lifting his horse off the ground, to come in just ahead of the other two riders.

It was, she knew, by sheer determination that he had been so successful.

Once again she took the cheque for 250 pounds before anyone else could snatch it from him.

Then they went to the Castle for Luncheon.

It was a noisy meal.

Everyone teased Harry for being so successful.

Charles was complaining that he had so many demands on his money from beautiful women that he would be fortunate if he was left at the end of the day with half-a-crown.

He was only joking, but Amorita felt in her pocket to make certain that Harry's cheques were still there.

After Luncheon, when the women went to change into their riding-habits, she hid the cheques in her bedroom.

She put them in a handkerchief, and hid it in the pocket of one of the day-gowns.

The first race of the afternoon was the one in which Harry was to ride *Mercury*.

He was a smaller horse than *Crusader*, but wiry-looking.

Amorita knew Harry would not have chosen him unless he thought he was particularly fast.

He proved this by coming in two lengths ahead of the rest of the field.

The same performance took place with Amorita taking the cheque.

Then she went to find *Hussar*, who had not

been on the race-course in the morning.

She found him being held with some difficulty by two grooms.

To their surprise, she insisted upon holding him herself.

" 'E be dang'rous when 'e's loike this!" one of the grooms said.

"Not with me," Amorita replied.

She talked to *Hussar* in the soft, gentle voice she had talked to him before.

He twitched his ears and even nuzzled against her, and she knew he was listening.

When she was in the saddle she walked him round quietly while the other race was taking place.

Harry had not taken part in this, feeling it would be unfair when he had won the two main races.

Amorita could see that he was surrounded by women paying him compliments and making a fuss of him.

She wondered if they were interested because of what they thought was in his pocket or because he was an attractive man.

"They may have good parts on the stage," she told herself, "but in real life they are really rather horrible!"

She did not want to be critical, but their behaviour at Luncheon had been almost as bad as it had been the night before.

She did not understand half the things they said, and they even shouted at the men.

Now she concentrated on getting *Hussar* to the starting-post.

When she arrived, the Earl said to her a little anxiously:

"You are all right? He is not going to be too much for you?"

"He is behaving like an angel," Amorita replied.

"In which case, you have obviously put a spell on him," the Earl answered, "and if you are not careful, you will be burned as a Witch!"

Amorita laughed.

However, he rode a little nearer to her to say:

"Do not take any chances, and if he is pulling you too hard, give him his head."

Amorita just smiled at him.

The Earl then said, as if he had just thought of it:

"I have a feeling that you ride rather like Harry, and if you are as good as he is, then I need not worry."

"I shall be all right," Amorita replied.

As she said the last words, she realised that Zena had come up beside her and was looking at her speculatively.

"I hope you've got my prize ready for me, Roydin!" she said to the Earl. "This horse is magnificent, and I only hope it doesn't get

obstructed by 'small fry' as don't know how
to ride!"

She was, Amorita knew, being unnecessarily
rude, so she rode away.

The Earl rounded them up.

There was some delay at the starting-point
because *Hussar* wanted to start off before the
rest of the field.

"If you can't control the horse, then you
shouldn't take part in the race," Zena said
spitefully.

"He is just a little over-eager to win," Amorita
said quietly.

"As that's highly unlikely," Zena retorted,
"you'd be wise to take him back to the stables."

Amorita did not deign to answer.

A minute later the Earl gave the signal, and
they were off.

Amorita deliberately, as her Father had always
taught her, drew in *Hussar* at the beginning.

She held him back from rushing ahead as he
wished to do.

She was talking to him as she did so.

After nearly pulling her arms from her body,
she thought he understood.

When they had gone round twice, there were
still three women in front of her, one of them
being Zena.

It was only when they reached the last part of
the field that she gave *Hussar* his head.

As if he understood exactly what she wanted, he took off like a pistol-shot.

All Amorita had to do was to keep in the saddle and let him carry her to the winning-post.

He passed it two lengths ahead of the others amid cheers from the on-lookers.

When she went to accept her prize, the Earl said:

"I do not need to tell you that you rode brilliantly!"

"I can only thank you for letting me ride what I thought was the fastest horse in your stable," Amorita said quietly.

He gave her the cheque, saying:

"Perhaps this will enable you to pay for a twin to *Hussar*."

Amorita thought that was what she would dream of owning.

But there were far more important things needed at home.

When they went back to the Castle, Zena was being spiteful and extremely rude, but she did not listen.

All she was thinking of was that for the first time in her life she would be able to contribute to the upkeep of her home, and not be a burden on Harry.

He had said to her at Luncheon:

"When we come back after the race, if you take my advice, you will lie down. After all that excitement, you are bound to be tired."

"That goes for you too," Amorita replied.

"We will both rest," Harry promised with a smile. "Tea will undoubtedly be just more champagne, and we can keep that for the evening."

"You are drinking too much," Amorita said in a low voice. "You know it does not suit you."

"I agree," Harry answered. "I had better not have too much if I am to ride to-morrow before we leave."

Amorita realised he had given up the idea of leaving soon after the races.

She knew, when Harry thought about it, that it would be rude to leave after they had won so much.

There was also the parade before the dinner-party, which the Earl was thinking of as a tremendous triumph to the end of a successful day.

She went to her bedroom and found Mrs. Dawson there.

"I won the race!" she said, feeling she must tell someone of her success.

"So I hears," Mrs. Dawson answered, "and they're saying downstairs what an outstanding rider you are, Miss. It's something I never expected!"

"I learned to ride as soon as I left the cradle," Amorita replied.

Mrs. Dawson started to say something, but changed her mind, and instead she asked:

"What are you wearing to-night, Miss?"

"Oh—anything," Amorita answered. "I am sure there must be several gowns I have not yet worn."

Mrs. Dawson looked at her in surprise.

"But the other young women," she said, "are all in Fancy-Dress!"

"Fancy-Dress?" Amorita exclaimed. "I had no idea of that!"

"Well, I gathers they concocted it amongst themselves before they left London, and thought they'd give the men something to talk about—as if they needed it!"

There was a sharp note in Mrs. Dawson's voice, and Amorita said:

"I am afraid I have no Fancy-Dress, so perhaps I need not compete."

"That'd upset His Lordship's plans," Mrs. Dawson replied. "I was thinking while I was waiting for you that there's some Fancy-Dress costumes put away from the old days when Her Ladyship was alive—God rest her soul."

"You have some here?" Amorita asked. "Oh, please, could I borrow one?"

"I can find you something that'll suit you very much better than what you're wearing," Mrs. Dawson said, "but now you have to go to sleep, Miss. I'll have it ready for you when you wakes."

"Oh, thank you, thank you!" Amorita said. "You are so kind to me and I am very grateful."

"I can't think how your parents allow you to do what you're doing now!" Mrs. Dawson said.

Amorita thought she was referring to her being on the stage, and she said quickly:

"My parents are both dead, and you will understand I have no money."

"That's what I suspected," Mrs. Dawson remarked. "At the same time, there must be something else you could do?"

"If there is, I have not yet discovered what it is," Amorita said somewhat apologetically.

Mrs. Dawson pressed her lips together as if she would prevent herself from saying what she thought.

Then, as Amorita got into bed, she said:

"It's a pity—a real pity—that's all I can say!"

She pulled the curtains and went from the room without saying any more.

Amorita smiled to herself.

'Nanny would say exactly the same!' she thought.

Because she was worrying about what was happening at the Hospital, she did not think any more about herself.

chapter six

WHEN Amorita looked at herself in the mirror, she laughed.

"No-one will expect me to look like this," she said.

"It's how you should look, Miss," Mrs. Dawson replied, "and if you want me to tell you the truth, you looks very lovely."

Amorita looked at herself again.

Mrs. Dawson had brought from upstairs the costume which the Earl's Mother had worn in a Play that had been put on in the Castle at Christmas.

It was the clothes and wings of an Angel.

The soft white of the robe and the wings made from the feathers of a swan were certainly unusual.

Before she had allowed her to look at herself,

Mrs. Dawson had arranged Amorita's hair close to her head.

She had then placed at the back a golden halo.

Amorita certainly looked very different from how she had in the gowns that had been lent her by Milly.

It flashed through her mind that perhaps Harry would be annoyed.

Then she told herself she had a choice.

She could come to the party in an ordinary gown, or in Fancy-Dress, if an unusual one.

She knew Mrs. Dawson was waiting for her approval, and she said:

"Thank you, dear Mrs. Dawson. You have been so kind to me. It is difficult to know what to say, but I am very, very grateful."

"If you asks me," Mrs. Dawson said, "you looks as you should, while those gowns are only fit for them as lives in London."

There was a scathing note in her voice which said better than words that she disapproved of the other women in the party.

Amorita thought, however, that it would be a mistake for her to be involved in criticising anybody.

She therefore said:

"I feel rather shy of going downstairs, but I do not suppose anybody will notice me particularly."

Mrs. Dawson was not listening.

She was taking from a box a doll which she place in Amorita's arms.

"Now, that's what you should carry," she said.

Amorita looked down at the doll questioningly.

It was wrapped in a shawl so that when she held it in her arms the face could not be clearly seen.

She could imagine all too well the rude remarks that Zena would make.

Then she asked herself why should she worry?

She thanked Mrs. Dawson again.

As the gong sounded downstairs to tell the women they were expected in the Ball-Room, she went to the door.

The Earl had said that the women were not to be seen until they appeared on the stage.

He had therefore arranged for the men, which included himself, to be seated in the Ball-Room before the first "Incomparable" appeared.

When Amorita came downstairs, a footman hurried her down a passage to the back of the Ball-Room.

There was a door leading into an Ante-room where the women were all congregating.

They were wearing, Amorita saw at a glance, a variety of strange or outrageous costumes.

She was not really surprised to see that Zena was dressed as a Snake-Charmer.

Her gown was very scanty.

She had a small snake with glittering eyes round her neck, another round her naked waist, and an even larger one in her hands.

She was talking to Lou-Lou, who was dressed as Pierrot with a large curly wig on her head, and her make-up accentuated.

As Lou-Lou had beautiful legs, she certainly looked striking, if somewhat outrageous.

As Amorita went into the Ante-room, a servant handed her a number.

She knew it was the order in which she was to appear.

It was Eleven, which meant there was only one woman to come after her.

She therefore thought there was no hurry and hoping no-one would notice her, she moved towards the window.

It opened into the garden.

She slipped outside, thinking this was a moment when she might look at the fountain.

It was something she had longed to do.

She only had a glimpse of it before Harry had hurried her away.

Behind her, she heard the music being played as the first "Incomparable" walked onto the stage.

There was the sound of clapping, and she hurried into the dusk.

The fountain was even more beautiful than she had thought.

The bowl was very ancient and carved.

The water came through the mouth of a dolphin being held by Cupid.

It was thrown high into the sky, glittering in the last dying light of the setting sun.

It appeared to Amorita like prayers going up to Heaven.

Suddenly she became aware that a man was standing beside her.

"It's sorry Oi am t'be late, Ma'am," he said breathlessly. "But Oi lorst me way. 'Ere's wot ye ordered, an' the Master says one drop an' ye be drunk, two an' ye be drunk as a Lord, free, an' yer out—cold!"

He spoke with a broad Cockney accent.

It was made stronger by the fact that he was breathless, as if he had been running.

Then, as he thrust something into Amorita's hand, she realised it was a small bottle.

As he did so, a sharp voice said:

"That's for me!"

The bottle was snatched from her by Zena.

Before Amorita could say anything, she turned to the Cockney, saying angrily:

"Where the devil have you been? I expected you an hour ago!"

"Oi knows—Oi knows!" the man said. "But Oi couldn' find th' place."

While he was speaking, Amorita moved quickly away.

She had no wish to be involved with Zena, whom she knew would be rude to her.

It was unfortunate that the Cockney had confused their identities.

Going round the other side of the fountain, she saw the Rose Garden ahead, and looked back.

The fountain was deserted.

There was no sign of Zena, nor the Cockney.

"I wonder what he brought her?" Amorita asked herself.

Then the words he had said came back to her mind.

It suddenly struck her that the bottle she had held for a moment in her hand must have contained some sort of drug.

What had he said?

"One drop and you are drunk, two and you are drunk as a Lord. Three and you are out cold!"

'I am sure she is going to do something horrible to somebody!' Amorita thought.

Then, because Zena was a companion of Sir Mortimer's, she was sure it was something to do with money.

Who, she asked herself, were they intending to drug?

Could it be someone like Harry, who had three cheques they had not been able to get into their hands?

Thank goodness she had hidden the cheques

where no-one would find them!

At the same time, she was frightened.

She had a sudden urge to go back to her room and hide them somewhere else.

As she hurried towards the Castle, another idea came into her mind.

The only person in the party who would really have enough money was the Earl himself.

Could Zena be contemplating drugging him?

It seemed such an unlikely and almost absurd idea that she wanted to dismiss it from her mind.

Yet she kept thinking how rich the Earl was!

Zena had tried to get Harry to give her some of his winnings.

"I must warn him!" she told herself.

She could hear the sounds of clapping coming through the open window of the Ball-Room.

When finally she went into the Ante-room she found there were only four women left.

"Where have you been?" one of them asked. "I thought you'd miss your turn."

"I wanted to look at the fountain," Amorita replied truthfully.

She was relieved to find that Zena had already gone out onto the stage.

"Well, you looks very pretty," the woman she was speaking to said, "but I don't know as an Angel's the sort of person you'd expect t'find at this party!"

The other women laughed.

"If I'd have thought of it, I'd have come as the Devil himself!" one said.

"Don't worry," another answered, "Zena's playing that part, and you can be sure someone's going to burn in Hell!"

They laughed again.

Then the next number was called and the woman who had just spoken hurried onto the stage.

When it came to Amorita's turn, she could feel the "butterflies," as she called them, fluttering in her breast.

She had been peeping through the door that led onto the stage.

The woman in front of her had twirled round, then kicked her legs high above her head.

It evoked a roar of applause from the men watching.

Amorita was thankful that she need do nothing but just walk on quietly.

If they did not applaud her, it would not matter one way or the other.

There were cries of "Do it again!" as Number Ten walked off the stage and into the audience.

As if the Band was aware that Amorita was different, the music was very soft as a footman on the door announced:

"Number Eleven!"

Slowly, because she was shy and also she felt it was correct, Amorita walked onto the small stage.

She was holding the doll in her arms, and she stood very still, looking down at it.

She had no idea that the lights the Earl had arranged made her halo gleam brightly.

Her face on which she had put only a little make-up was sweet, gentle, and at the same time, beautiful.

Just for a moment there was complete silence.

Every actor knows that is the greatest tribute an audience can pay him.

Then, as serenely as Amorita had entered, she walked back towards the Ante-room.

The applause was almost deafening.

She thought it would be a mistake for her to join the noisy audience.

She just stood, getting her breath back and feeling relieved it was all over.

Number Twelve was being called.

The music started up a very different tune.

Amorita walked across the room and went to the window to breathe in the evening air.

As she put the doll down on a chair, Harry joined her.

He came hurrying in, saying as he reached her:

"You were wonderful! Where did that get-up come from? I am sure it was not in the trunks."

"Mrs. Dawson found it for me," Amorita answered, "otherwise I would not have had a Fancy-Dress."

"I know. I learned about it only at the last minute," Harry admitted, "and I was wondering what you would do. But you were marvellous, and very different from the others."

"I was afraid," Amorita said, "you might be angry because I was."

"No, no," he said in a low voice. "It was quite all right."

Amorita glanced over her shoulder, then she said:

"There is something I want to tell you."

Before she could speak, the Earl came into the room from the stage door to say:

"Rita, you have won! There is no question about it—the votes were almost unanimous!"

Amorita gave a little gasp.

"I . . . I do not . . . believe it!"

"It is true," the Earl said. "Now, here is a thousand pounds for you, Harry, and something very special for Rita."

As he was talking, a number of men and some of the women came crowding in.

"What are you giving her?" Zena asked jealously.

She was almost the first to appear.

Amorita saw Harry quickly put what the Earl had given him into the inside pocket of his evening-coat.

Because the Earl was waiting, Amorita opened

the large jewel-box he had put into her hand.

Lying on a bed of velvet was an exquisite, and what she thought was a very expensive, diamond necklace.

She looked at it in astonishment.

Without thinking, she exclaimed:

"But . . . I cannot accept . . . this!"

"Of course you can," the Earl said. "I have never met a woman yet who did not like diamonds."

Amorita wanted to expostulate, as she knew it would have shocked her Mother.

She had always said that no Lady ever accepted jewels from a man, certainly nothing as expensive as the diamond necklace.

At that moment she felt Harry pinch her arm, and she remembered who she was supposed to be.

An actress like Zena—would of course accept anything she was offered.

Harry took the necklace out of the box and put it round Amorita's neck.

He fastened it, and she said to the Earl:

"Thank . . . you . . . thank you . . . very much!"

"I thought it would please you," he answered, "and now let us go in to dinner."

He offered his arm to Amorita.

She took it thinking that because she had won the competition, he was merely being polite.

Only when she was seated on his right at the

dinner table did she realise that Zena was on his left and must therefore have been voted second.

The wine was flowing and everybody seemed to be talking at once.

The women in their strange costumes certainly made the table look very festive.

The food was delicious.

But because everyone was drinking so much, Amorita was sure they did not appreciate what they were eating.

She glanced down the table at Harry and hoped he would keep to his resolution not to drink.

'If we can ride to-morrow before we leave,' she thought, 'it would be wonderful! Especially if I can have *Hussar*!'

Course succeeded course, and glasses were filled and refilled.

As the dinner was nearing its end, Zena suddenly turned to the Earl and said:

"I've got a surprise for you, Roydin, and one I think you'll enjoy."

"What is it?" the Earl asked rather absently.

He was watching a couple further down the table who were kissing each other passionately.

He wondered if in doing so they would upset their glasses.

Amorita was thinking the same thing.

She also considered their behaviour extremely vulgar.

"What I've got for you," she heard Zena saying, "is a love-potion and a very special one from a recipe left me by my Grandmother."

"I do not think I need a love-potion," the Earl said with an amused smile.

"But you'll try it—just to please me?" Zena begged.

Amorita had only been listening vaguely while she watched the couple at the end of the table.

Now it occurred to her that Zena was about to drug the Earl.

She would give him what was in the bottle which the Cockney had brought her.

'If she can make him very drunk,' she thought, 'she will perhaps be able to get some money out of him.'

She saw now that Zena had a small bottle on the table in front of her.

"I'm giving you only a little," she was saying.

She lifted the bottle and poured some of what she had called a "love-potion" into a liqueur glass.

Amorita knew that somehow she had to prevent the Earl from drinking it.

She pulled at her diamond necklace and it fell onto the floor.

As it did so, she gave a cry.

"My necklace! Oh, please, My Lord, pick it up for me."

The Earl bent down between their two chairs,

and as he did so, she whispered so that only he could hear:

"Do not drink what she is giving you. It is a drug!"

The Earl heard what she said.

He straightened himself, and held out the diamond necklace.

"Let me fasten it for you," he said.

She bent her head and he fastened it behind her halo.

As his fingers touched her skin, a strange feeling she could not explain ran through her.

Then he said:

"Now, be careful not to lose your prize again, or it might vanish!"

"And if it . . . did?" Amorita asked.

"I would have to buy you another!" he replied.

He laughed as if at his own joke.

As he turned back in his chair his hand knocked over the glass that Zena had filled.

It spilled onto the table.

"I am sorry," he exclaimed. "How clumsy of me!"

A footman behind his chair hurried to clear up the mess with a napkin.

"I'll give you another glass," Zena said.

But the Earl apparently did not hear her.

He rose to his feet, saying:

"I think now we will go into the Drawing-Room, where you will find there is gambling to amuse you, or, if you prefer, the Band is playing in the Ball-Room."

Everyone began to talk at once, deciding where they would go.

Amorita realised that as they rose from their chairs some of the men were very unsteady.

Harry was not sitting next to her, but she thought he would understand if she slipped away.

She therefore moved with the others towards the door.

When they entered the hall she hurried up the stairs.

As she reached the landing she looked back.

She saw Zena moving in her usual seductive manner with the bottle in both her hands.

'At least I have saved the Earl from that!' she thought as she hurried into her bedroom.

She was not surprised to find Mrs. Dawson there, delighted that she had won first prize.

The Housekeeper helped Amorita out of the angel robes.

Having removed the halo, she then insisted on brushing Amorita's hair.

"They've all been saying below stairs how you looks like an Angel yourself, Miss," Mrs. Dawson said. "You're too good for the likes of this lot, and that's the truth."

Amorita was inclined to agree with her, but she did not say so.

She only thanked Mrs. Dawson again.

She got into bed, but she did not turn out the light.

She felt she was too excited to sleep.

She thought instead how very, very lucky they were to have won so much money.

Because she was half-afraid it might have vanished like Fairy Gold, she got out of bed.

She went to the drawer where she had hidden it.

Then she looked at the necklace, wondering how much she could get for it.

"It is *mine*," she told herself proudly, "but whatever I sold it for, I would spend the money carefully so that never again are we in the position we were before we came here."

It sounded all right.

However, she knew it would be difficult to make the money last, seeing how much there was to do.

The operation for Nanny had to be paid for immediately.

But she was happier than she had ever been in her whole life.

Unexpectedly there was a knock on the door.

Before she could answer, it opened and the Earl came in.

"What is . . . it?" she asked.

"I am afraid you will be upset," he answered, "but Harry has passed out. I have had him taken to his room and my Valet is undressing him."

"Passed out?" Amorita exclaimed.

She did not wait to ask any more.

She opened the communicating door and went into Harry's room.

The Earl's Valet and a footman had laid him out on the bed.

Now they were taking off his shoes and coat.

Amorita was looking at her brother.

She saw that his eyes were closed, and he was completely unconscious.

Then, as the Valet laid his evening-coat on a chair, she had an idea.

She went to it and put her hand into the inside pocket.

It was empty!

She turned towards the Earl, who had followed her.

"This is Zena's doing!" she said. "She has drugged Harry as she intended to drug you, and has taken the thousand pounds you gave him!"

She spoke in a low voice because she did not want to make a scene in front of the servants.

As if the Earl understood, he drew her back into her own bedroom.

"How did you know that was what she was going to give me," he asked, "and how do you know that Harry has been drugged?"

In a low voice Amorita told him what had

happened when she was at the fountain.

She realised the Earl was looking at her incredulously.

Then there was an expression of anger on his face.

Without saying anything, he turned and walked from the room.

Amorita went back to Harry and now the two servants had got him into bed.

He was lying very still with the sheets covering him.

"I thinks he'll be all right, Miss," the Valet said, "but if ye wants me, the night-footman will fetch me from me room."

"Thank you very much," Amorita answered.

When the servants had left, she put her hand on Harry's forehead.

It was not very hot and she was sure the drug had not affected him as if he had been drinking.

"How could anybody do anything so vile?" she asked herself.

Leaving the communicating door open, she went back into her own room.

This was certainly not what she had expected after what had been a strange, but at the same time, exciting adventure.

'If Harry is well enough, we will leave to-morrow morning,' she thought. 'I cannot meet Zena again!'

She went once again to see that he had not

moved since she had left him.

Then she got into bed.

She did not blow out the lights, thinking that if he made a sound, or moved, she would be able to get to him at once.

It was a little later when there was a knock on the door and the Earl came in.

He had something in his hand, and he came to the side of the bed and put it down in front of Amorita.

She saw at a glance that it was the cheque Harry had received when she had come in first in the competition of the "Incomparables."

"You have got it back!" she exclaimed.

"I have got it back!" the Earl said in a hard voice. "And two other cheques they had managed to extract from men who were either too drunk or too drugged to stop them."

He did not wait for Amorita to say anything, but went on:

"I have ordered them both to leave my house immediately, and I shall see that Martin is thrown out of Whites Club!"

"I am so glad that I . . . saved you," Amorita said, "but I . . . never thought of her . . . doing anything . . . to . . . Harry!"

"He will be all right," the Earl said. "I have heard of this drug before. It wears off in twenty-four hours, although he may have a headache in the morning."

As he spoke, he sat down on the side of the bed.

"And now, Rita," he said, "what are we going to do about us?"

Amorita looked at him in surprise.

"I mean," the Earl said, "that I won you in the competition, and now I am going to tell you what I intend to do about you."

Amorita could only stare at him as he went on:

"I will buy you one of the most attractive houses in Chelsea, or St. John's Wood, if you prefer. I promise you shall have the best horses in London, both to ride and to drive. As for your necklace, I will give you far better jewellery than that!"

"I . . . I do not . . . understand . . . what you . . . are saying!" Amorita protested.

Because she was obviously puzzled, the Earl explained:

"The conditions I made at this party were that every one of my men-friends would bring me the most attractive and beautiful 'Incomparable' in London because I did not have time to find them for myself."

"I . . . I am . . . sure that . . . Harry was not . . . aware of that," Amorita said. "And h-how could I possibly . . . accept all those . . . things from you?"

"Very easily," the Earl replied, "and I am sure

we shall be extremely happy together."

He smiled at her, then he said in a different tone of voice:

"You are very lovely! I knew the moment you arrived that you were different from any other woman here."

He paused and then continued:

"I am sorry about Harry, but I cannot wait to tell you how much I want you, and how much you mean to me. Will you come to my room, or shall we stay here?"

It was then Amorita understood what he meant.

She recoiled from him, saying:

"No, no . . . of course . . . not! How . . . can you . . . imagine I could do . . . such a thing? I . . . I did not . . . know that . . . those . . . women were . . . l-like . . . that!"

The Earl stared at her.

"You—did not know? Then what are you? Where do you come from?"

Quickly Amorita remembered what Harry had told her.

"I am . . . I am . . . an actress," she said, "although I have . . . not yet . . . had a part on . . . the st-stage."

"An actress!" the Earl said as if it were something he had never heard of before. "Then— Harry was breaking the rules!"

"Oh, please . . . you must not be angry with

him," Amorita said. "The friend he was bringing let him down and . . . because I felt . . . sorry for him . . . I offered to come in her . . . place."

"I see!" the Earl said slowly, working it out in his mind. "And I suppose they are her clothes you are wearing—which do not really suit you."

"Y-yes . . . that is . . . right," Amorita answered.

She was terrified that the Earl might say that as Harry had broken the rules, he would have to give back the money he had won.

She therefore said pleadingly:

"Please . . . please . . . do not be . . . angry with . . . Harry! He did so . . . want to . . . ride in the races . . . and I had to . . . fight to . . . persuade him that if I . . . came there . . . would be . . . no difficulty."

The Earl was looking at her, she thought, in a strange way.

Then he said:

"I suppose what you are really telling me," he said, "is that you are in love with Harry, and have no wish to leave him."

"I do . . . love him!" Amorita agreed.

The Earl sighed.

"Very well," he said. "The party has ended in a rather different manner from what I expected, but, of course, as Harry has been knocked out, you must look after him."

"Thank . . . you for . . . being so . . . understanding," Amorita whispered.

"I have never done anything quite so difficult in my whole life," the Earl said. "To be frank, Rita, you have spoilt my party for me."

"I . . . I am s-sorry."

Amorita looked up at him pleadingly.

Then, before she could be aware of it, the Earl bent forward and kissed her.

It was a very gentle kiss, but Amorita had never been kissed before.

It flashed through her mind that it was what she expected a kiss would be, but somehow more wonderful.

Just for a moment, the Earl held her close.

Then in a hoarse voice he said:

"Good-night, Rita."

He rose from the bed and walked to the door.

He did not look back, but went out, shutting it quietly behind him.

chapter seven

AMORITA lay back against the pillows, thinking the whole world had turned upside-down.

For a moment she could feel nothing but the thrills that ran through her when the Earl kissed her.

Then she remembered what he had said.

It was as if there were a flaming light in front of her eyes.

He had asked her to become his mistress.

Amorita was very innocent and knew very little about men.

But she was well-educated.

She had read, of course, about the mistresses of Charles II and those of the French King, Louis XIV.

But it had never crossed her mind for one moment that the women at the Earl's party were not actresses, as she had believed.

Now she knew they were the mistresses of the men who had brought them.

She could understand why Harry had been so reluctant to take her in place of Milly, why he had tried to protect her from too close a contact with Zena and the other women.

She thought of the Earl, then said in a whisper:

"How . . . could he . . . think I would . . . do . . . anything like . . . that?"

With a shudder she realised that he now believed she was Harry's mistress.

She sat up in bed in a panic.

"We must leave . . . we must leave . . . at once! How can I ever face . . . him, or those . . . women again?"

She got out of bed and walked into Harry's bed-room.

He was still unconscious.

For a moment she had the terrifying feeling that he might be dead.

Because she was frightened, she felt his heart.

It was beating steadily, and when she touched his forehead it was still comparatively cool.

She went back to bed and made plans.

She must have dozed a little, for when she woke with a start she was aware there had been a noise in Harry's room.

She ran in and found that he had moved in

the bed and was turning his head from side to side.

His eyes were closed and she was sure he was still deeply drugged.

She looked at the clock on the mantelpiece and saw that it was nearly four o'clock.

That meant the dawn would be breaking.

She went back into her own room and dressed herself.

She had to put on the gown in which she had arrived at the Castle.

But she told herself she would leave the other clothes Milly had given her behind.

She never wanted to see them again.

When she was dressed she went down the stairs to find the night-porter.

It was very quiet.

Even so, she walked softly, afraid of disturbing anybody.

The night-porter was dozing in the padded leather chair which must have stood in the hall for centuries.

She woke him and said slowly, so that he could not make a mistake:

"Will you please go to the stables and ask for the Phaeton in which Sir Edward Howe arrived."

"Ye're leavin', Ma'am?" the night-porter enquired.

"Yes," Amorita replied. "Sir Edward has been taken ill and I have to get him to a Doctor."

The night-porter seemed to understand.

Then, as she turned towards the stairs, Amorita said:

"When the Phaeton comes round, will you get somebody to help you carry Sir Edward downstairs and lift him into it?"

The night-porter looked surprised, but he answered:

"Oi'll do that, Ma'am."

He hurried out through the front-door, and Amorita went back to her room.

She sat down at the *secrétaire* which stood in a corner of the bedroom and wrote a note to Mrs. Dawson.

In her elegant hand-writing she began:

Dear Mrs. Dawson,
Thank you for being so kind
and helpful to me. I have taken
Sir Edward home so that he can see
a Doctor.
Will you please give, or throw
away the clothes I have left behind,
and give His Lordship the necklace
which is on the dressing-table.
Thank you again.

Yours sincerely,
Rita Reele.

She left the letter on the bed so that Mrs. Dawson could not fail to see it.

Quickly she collected the few things that were her own into a bundle.

She carefully put the cheques she had hidden into her hand-bag, also the one the Earl had retrieved from Zena.

Then she remembered that she should tip the night-porter.

She went into Harry's room.

To her relief, she found some small change in the pocket of his evening coat.

As she looked at it, she realised that the one thing she must not leave behind were Harry's clothes.

Hastily, she dragged his case from a cupboard.

She started putting into it everything she could find that belonged to him.

She was still doing this when the night-porter and a footman he must have woken up came into the room.

"Oi'll do that, Miss," the footman said.

Amorita gave a sigh of relief.

She went back into her own bedroom to collect the cape she had worn when she arrived.

She looked at the bonnet with its fluttering feathers and decided she would not wear it.

At this hour no-one would think she looked strange.

She looked round to see if she had forgotten anything.

She could think only of how the Earl had sat on her bed last night!

He had bent forward to kiss her.

Just for a moment she felt again that magical quiver in her breast.

Then she remembered that he thought he was kissing Harry's mistress.

Quickly she ran back into Harry's room.

The men had packed everything he possessed and were now wrapping him in blankets to carry him down the stairs.

"Be very careful," Amorita said.

"Don' 'ee worry, Ma'am, us'll not drop 'im," the night-porter answered.

Slowly, with Amorita following them, they went down the stairs, step by step, until they reached the hall.

Through the open front-door, Amorita could see the Phaeton which belonged to Charlie.

His two perfectly matched horses were between the shafts.

There was a groom holding them.

When Amorita climbed into the driving-seat, he said in surprise:

"Be ye a-goin' t'drive it, Miss?"

"Yes, I am," Amorita answered, "and I am sure I will have no difficulty with these horses."

The groom looked doubtful.

Amorita turned to where the footmen had placed Harry on the seat beside her.

His head was on a pillow and they were tucking some thick blankets round him.

He was obviously still unconscious and had not the slightest idea of what was happening to him.

Amorita tipped the three men.

Then, picking up the reins, she drove off.

As they went down the drive, she wanted to look back at the Castle.

She would never see it again, just as she would never see the Earl again.

"He must . . . never know who I am . . . really because it would . . . hurt Harry," she told herself. "He will forget . . . me, but I will . . . never . . . forget . . . him!"

She knew, too, she would never forget her first kiss.

She had the frightening feeling that no other kiss would ever be so wonderful.

Then she concentrated on driving home as quickly as she could.

*　　*　　*

It took Amorita three hours to reach the entrance to their castle.

As she drove up the drive it certainly did not compare with the Castle she had just left.

It seemed very small and even more dilapidated than she remembered.

By now the sun was high in the Heavens.

It shone on the garden full of the flowers her Mother had loved.

"We are home!" she told herself. "And now there must be . . . no more . . . adventures . . . and we must . . . spend the money we have . . . won very . . . very . . . carefully."

She had thought when she was putting their winnings into her hand-bag that perhaps she ought to leave behind the thousand pounds the Earl had paid Harry for her.

Then she told herself practically that they needed every penny.

Anyway, the Earl would not understand because he would never know that she was not what he thought her to be.

She calculated that what was left of Harry's change would provide them with food until they could go to the Bank.

Then they could cash the 3,250 pounds they had won from the Earl.

As she drew up outside the front-door, she saw Ben coming from the direction of the stables.

"Ye be 'ome, Miss Am'rita!" he said unnecessarily.

"Yes, Ben, and you can put the horses in the stables, but first I want you to help me take Sir Edward upstairs. He is not well."

On Amorita's instructions, Ben went into the Castle and collected Briggs and his wife.

It was quite a job, but somehow they managed to carry Harry up the stairs.

Amorita drove the Phaeton into the stable-yard.

She had taken the horses from between the shafts before Ben joined her.

"Them be a foine pair o' 'orses, Miss Am'rita!" Ben said.

"I enjoyed driving them," Amorita admitted. "Give them plenty to eat, Ben. I expect they are hungry."

"Oi'll see t'em," Ben said. " 'Tis a pity, when ye comes t'think on it, that we can't keep 'em."

"I agree with you," Amorita replied, "but unfortunately, they have to go back to Lord Raynam."

She walked towards the house as she spoke.

She knew that never again would she be driving such well-bred horses.

Never again would she ride *Hussar*.

She ran up the stairs and found that Harry was in bed, but his eyes were open.

"What—has been—happening? How did—I get—here?" he asked in a thick voice as Amorita joined him.

"I will tell you all about it later," she replied. "I expect at the moment you would like something to drink."

As she spoke, Mrs. Briggs came in with a glass in her hand.

"What have you got there?" Amorita asked.

" 'Tis honey, Miss."

Amorita looked surprised.

"Honey?" she questioned.

"Yer Mother always said that if a man's had too much t'drink, give 'im honey an' he'll soon be hisself again."

Amorita saw that Mrs. Briggs had mixed the honey with warm water.

To her surprise, Harry drank it without protest.

He lay back against the pillows.

"I have the hell of a headache!" he complained.

"Try to go back to sleep," Amorita advised, "and I expect it will soon go away."

"I'll put another glass beside th' bed," Mrs. Briggs said, "and persuade 'im to keep drinkin' it, Miss Amorita."

"I will," Amorita promised.

She went into her own bedroom.

She pulled off the elegant gown which Milly had given her and flung it on the floor.

She knew she would never wear it again and felt even to look at it upset her.

Instead, she put on one of her old white muslin gowns.

It had been washed a dozen times, but it made her feel more like herself.

"And *not*," she said scornfully to her reflection in the mirror, "like a . . . mistress."

The word seemed to haunt her.

Because she, too, was tired after a sleepless night and the long drive, she lay down on the sofa in the Drawing-Room.

Before she could go on thinking of the Earl, she fell asleep.

* * *

Amorita awoke with a start to find she had slept for hours.

She was sure it must be late in the afternoon.

She got up to find there was a note in Briggs's rough hand-writing which read:

Gone shops get food. Have given
Sir Harry something to eat.
                              Briggs.

Amorita hurried upstairs.

There was a tray by Harry's bed.

She saw that he had eaten quite a lot of what Mrs. Briggs had prepared for him.

He had also apparently drunk another glass of honey.

He was, however, asleep.

Amorita realised with a sense of relief that it was not the frightening unconsciousness in which she had brought him away from Castle Elde.

He was breathing naturally and the colour had returned to his face.

"He is better," she told herself, "and I expect he will be able to get up to-morrow."

She, too, felt very much better through having slept.

She tidied her hair, then realised that, because she had been away, there were no flowers in the Castle.

It was something which her Mother had always insisted on having.

"We may be poor and things may be shabby," she had said, "but flowers are always beautiful, and they make the dullest rooms look lovely."

Amorita went out into the garden.

She began to pick the flowers that were blooming in several flower-beds.

Even as she did so, she kept thinking of the fountain at the Castle.

How beautiful it had been in the fading light!

The basket she was carrying was nearly full.

She put it down for a moment by the little stream which her Father had made at the end of the garden.

It cascaded over some rocks where her Mother had grown some special rock-plants.

'We may not have a fountain,' Amorita thought with a little sigh, 'so I must be content with a small cascade.'

She thought the fountain was right for the Earl.

No-one, she thought, could look more

handsome than he when he was mounted on his black stallion.

And he had kissed her!

She could still feel the touch of his lips on hers.

Suddenly she was aware that she was not alone.

She turned round and, incredibly so that she gave a little gasp, he was standing behind her.

Her eyes met his.

For a long moment they were both very still, unable to move, unable to look away.

Then the Earl said in a deep voice:

"A groom told me I would find Miss *Amorita* in the garden!"

"B-But . . . why are you . . . h-here?" Amorita asked. "How can . . . you have . . . left your . . . p-party?"

"I told Charlie to take charge," the Earl replied, "and came to see what had happened to you, and, of course, to Harry."

"He is . . . b-better . . . m-much better . . ." Amorita stammered.

"And why did you not tell me he was your brother?" the Earl demanded.

Amorita gave a little cry.

"You must not . . . know that and if you . . . do you must never . . . tell anybody! Harry said if . . . it was known he had . . . taken me to . . . your party, he would be . . . thrown out of . . . Whites Club, and . . . many people would . . .

never speak to . . . him again."

"And yet you came with him!"

"I had . . . to," Amorita said. "We had to have some money . . . first to . . . pay for an . . . operation for our . . . old Nanny. Without it she . . . will die . . . and secondly . . . to keep . . . ourselves from . . . starving."

She thought the Earl looked incredulous, and she said quickly:

"Please . . . believe me . . . go away and . . . pretend you have . . . never seen . . . me."

The Earl smiled.

"Do you think that is possible?"

"It is . . . something you . . . must do if . . . you are . . . fond of . . . Harry."

"And you really think," the Earl said, "that you can hide the fact for ever that he has a sister?"

"He never . . . invites his friends . . . here," Amorita said, "because he . . . cannot . . . afford to . . . offer them the same . . . hospitality that . . . he is . . . given."

She clasped her hands together as she said:

"Please . . . please . . . go on being . . . friends with him. Let him . . . ride your horses . . . and do not . . . tell anybody about . . . m-me."

"I am making Harry manager of my race-horses," the Earl said, "and, of course, he will live at the Castle."

"How . . . wonderful!" Amorita gasped.

"Harry . . . will be thrilled. Can . . . you be so . . . kind . . . so . . . understanding?"

The words seemed to tumble over themselves, and there were tears in her eyes.

The Earl stood looking at her.

Then he asked in a low voice:

"What did you feel, Amorita, when I kissed you?"

Because she had not expected the question, she blushed and looked away from him.

The Earl came a little nearer.

"I want to know—I want you to tell me the truth," he said. "I may be wrong, but I had the feeling you had never been kissed before."

Amorita did not answer.

He reached out and took her chin in his hand and raised her face to his.

"Tell me!" he said persuasively. "Am I the first man to kiss you?"

Amorita was trembling because he was touching her.

He knew the answer without her telling him in words.

Then he pulled her closer to him and his lips took possession of hers.

He kissed her at first gently, then possessively and demandingly, as if he were making her his.

It was to Amorita as if the stars had fallen from the sky and were trembling in her breast.

The strange thrill that had run through her before increased a thousandfold.

She no longer felt that she was herself, but a part of the Earl.

The rest of the world had disappeared.

He kissed her and went on kissing her until she could no longer think, but only feel.

Then he raised his head.

"I love you!" he said. "I love you as I have never loved another woman. Now tell me what you feel about me."

"I . . . I love . . . you," Amorita whispered. "I love you . . . and I did not . . . know that love was . . . so wonderful!"

The Earl kissed her again.

Then he said:

"I could not believe that anyone existed who was so lovely, so perfect, until I saw you standing on the stage dressed as an Angel, and holding a baby in your arms. I wanted it to be my son."

It was then Amorita woke up to what they were doing.

"I . . . I should not . . . have been there," she stammered, "and . . . and you must . . . go away."

"I have no intention of doing that!" the Earl replied. "I am asking you to marry me, Amorita, and I know that nothing else in the world matters, except that you should be my wife."

For a moment Amorita's face seemed to be transformed.

She looked so beautiful that the Earl could

hardly believe she was real.

Then with a little cry she said:

"B-but . . . you know . . . I cannot . . . m-marry you."

"Why not?" the Earl asked.

"Because it will hurt . . . Harry . . . because your friends will of course . . . recognise me."

"We can be clever enough not to hurt Harry," the Earl said, "and when you are my wife, my Precious one, you will look very different from how you did in those gaudy clothes that did not suit you, and with all that paint and powder on your face."

Amorita hid her face against his shoulder.

"H-Harry said I . . . had to wear it . . . but I . . . I thought it was . . . because I was . . . supposed to be an . . . actress."

The Earl's eyes were very tender as he looked down at her.

"You may have to go on acting for a little while," he said, "but, when we have enjoyed a very long honeymoon and I have bought for you the most beautiful clothes obtainable, we are going to live in the country while we repair the Castle."

He looked at her to see if she was listening, and went on:

"The only people who will visit us at first will be our closest friends, like Charlie, Jimmy, and, of course, Harry. If the rest turn up very much later, it is doubtful if they will see any resemblance between the beautiful Countess of Eldridge and the young woman who called herself 'Rita Reele.' "

"Do . . . you mean . . . I *can* . . . marry you?"

"I mean you are *going* to marry me," the Earl said firmly. "You will have to help me, my Darling, to spend my fortune sensibly and not waste it on fast women and slow horses!"

Because the way he said it was so funny, Amorita laughed.

Then she said:

"I thought I would . . . never be able . . . to . . . ride *Hussar* . . . again."

"And did you think you would never see me again?"

She moved a little closer to him.

"I thought . . . all I would . . . have to . . . remember was . . . that you had . . . kissed me."

"I will kiss you a million times," the Earl said, "and make you remember every kiss!"

He sighed with sheer happiness as he asked:

"How is it possible that I should be lucky enough to find you—the Angel that has always been in my heart, but I never believed I would find as a real woman?"

Then he was kissing her again, kissing her until she felt as if the garden were whirling around them.

They were flying high into the sky.

She knew that everything she had dreamed of and longed for had come true.

Now she need no longer be afraid for the future.

The Earl, in his own way, would make everything run smoothly, and there would be no more problems, no more fear, and most important of all, she would no longer be alone.

"I love you . . . I love . . . you!" she whispered when the Earl raised his head.

As she looked up into his eyes, she knew they had both found the one thing in the world which was more important than anything else, more important than money, friends, or enemies, more important than their Castles.

It was Love, the Love of a man for a woman, when they belong to each other so completely that they are no longer two people, but one.

"I love . . . you!" Amorita said again.

Then, as the Earl's lips held hers captive, there was no further need for words.

ABOUT THE AUTHOR

Barbara Cartland, the world's most famous romantic novelist, who is also an historian, playwright, lecturer, political speaker and television personality, has now written over 607 books and sold over six hundred and twenty million copies all over the world.

She has also had many historical works published and has written four autobiographies as well as the biographies of her mother and that of her brother, Ronald Cartland, who was the first Member of Parliament to be killed in the last war. This book has a preface by Sir Winston Churchill and has just been republished with an introduction by Sir Arthur Bryant.

Love at the Helm, a novel written with the help and inspiration of the late Earl Mountbatten of Burma, Great Uncle of His Royal Highness, The

Prince of Wales, is being sold for the Mountbatten Memorial Trust.

She has broken the world record for the last nineteen years by writing an average of twenty-three books a year. In the *Guinness Book of World Records* she is listed as the world's top-selling author.

Miss Cartland in 1987 sang an Album of Love Songs with the Royal Philharmonic Orchestra.

In private life Barbara Cartland, who is a Dame of the Order of St. John of Jerusalem, Chairman of the St. John Council in Hertfordshire and Deputy President of the St. John Ambulance Brigade, has fought for better conditions and salaries for Midwives and Nurses.

She championed the cause for the Elderly in 1956 invoking a Government Enquiry into the "Housing Condition of Old People."

In 1962 she had the Law of England changed so that Local Authorities had to provide camps for their own Gypsies. This has meant that since then thousands and thousands of Gypsy children have been able to go to School, which they had never been able to do in the past, as their caravans were moved every twenty-four hours by the Police.

There are now fourteen camps in Hertfordshire and Barbara Cartland has her own Romany Gypsy Camp called Barbaraville by the Gypsies.

Her designs "Decorating with Love" are being sold all over the U.S.A. and the National Home

Fashions League made her, in 1981, "Woman of Achievement."

She is unique in that she was one and two in the Dalton list of Best Sellers, and one week had four books in the top twenty.

Barbara Cartland's book *Getting Older, Growing Younger* has been published in Great Britain and the U.S.A. and her fifth cookery book, *The Romance of Food*, is now being used by the House of Commons.

In 1984 she received at Kennedy Airport America's Bishop Wright Air Industry Award for her contribution to the development of aviation. In 1931 she and two R.A.F. Officers thought of, and carried, the first aeroplane-towed glider airmail.

During the War she was Chief Lady Welfare Officer in Bedfordshire, looking after 20,000 Servicemen and -women. She thought of having a pool of Wedding Dresses at the war office so a Service Bride could hire a gown for the day.

She bought 1,000 gowns without coupons for the A.T.S., the W.A.A.F.'s and the W.R.E.N.S. In 1945 Barbara Cartland received the Certificate of Merit from Eastern Command.

In 1964 Barbara Cartland founded the National Association for Health of which she is the President, as a front for all the Health Stores and for any product made as alternative medicine.

This is now a £65 million turnover a year, with one-third going in export.

In January 1968 she received *La Médeille de Vermeil de la Ville de Paris*. This is the highest award to be given in France by the City of Paris. She has sold 25 million books in France.

In March 1988 Barbara Cartland was asked by the Indian Government to open their Health Resort outside Delhi. This is almost the largest Health Resort in the world.

Barbara Cartland was received with great enthusiasm by her fans, who feted her at a reception in the City, and she received the gift of an embossed plate from the Government.

Barbara Cartland was made a Dame of the Order of the British Empire in the 1991 New Year's Honours List by Her Majesty, The Queen, for her contribution to Literature and also for her years of work for the community.

Dame Barbara has now written 607 books, the greatest number of books by a British author, passing the 564 books written by John Creasey.

AWARDS

1945   Received Certificate of Merit, Eastern Command, for being Welfare Officer to 5,000 troops in Bedfordshire.

1953   Made a Commander of the Order of St. John of Jerusalem. Invested by H.R.H. The Duke of Gloucester at Buckingham Palace.

1972   Invested as Dame of Grace of the Order of St. John in London by The Lord Prior, Lord Cacia.

1981   Received "Achiever of the Year" from the National Home Furnishing Association in Colorado Springs, U.S.A., for her designs for wallpaper and fabrics.

1984   Received Bishop Wright Air Industry Award at Kennedy Airport, for inventing the aeroplane-towed Glider.

1988   Received from Monsieur Chirac, The Prime Minister, The Gold Medal of the City of Paris, at the Hotel de la Ville, Paris, for selling 25 million books and giving a lot of employment.

1991   Invested as Dame of the Order of The British Empire, by H.M. The Queen at Buckingham Palace for her contribution to Literature.